The plesiosaur surfaced underneath the skimming boat. The foils on the starboard side raked across its armored back and the craft tipped, lost flotation and crashed into water.

Chalfin had moved instinctively with the first turbulence. He cut the switches, held the boat up for a second or two as the water slowed its speed; and instead of a crashing capsize the upset was almost gentle.

Damn! he thought. Damn stupid clumsy lizard.

There was a swirl of water beside him. A snaky neck curled above him. A horrid beaked face looked into his own. Yellow eyes gleamed. The beak opened and closed, and Chalfin felt a sudden blinding pain that turned instantly to darkness. He never knew that the saurian had decapitated him or that he was dead.

MEET THE AUTHOR

Donald F. Glut was born in 1944 in Pecos, Texas, but was raised in Chicago, Illinois. He migrated to Los Angeles where, in 1967, he received a bachelor of arts degree in Cinema from the University of Southern California. While living in California, Glut worked as a musician, singer and actor.

Since becoming a writer in 1966, Glut has authored a score of books, including such novels as *Frankenstein Lives Again!* and *Bugged!*, as well as nonfiction works like *The Dinosaur Dictionary, The Frankenstein Legend, The Dracula Book, True Vampires of History, The Great Movie Serials* and *The Great Television Heroes* (the latter two with Jim Harmon). He is the creator of the comic book series *Dagar the Invincible, The Occult Files of Dr. Spektor* and *Tragg and the Sky Gods*, one of the regular writers of the *Tarzan* comic books and has written scripts for the *Shazam!* and *Land of the Lost* television programs. *Spawn* is his first LASER book.

DONALD GLUT

SPAWN

Cover
Illustration by
**KELLY
FREAS**

Toronto • New York • London

SPAWN

A LASER BOOK/first published October 1976

Copyright © 1976 by Donald Glut

ISBN 0-373 72043-2

Printed in the U.S.A.

PROLOGUE

Twin suns dawned above the rust-hued mountains at the world. Their radiance pierced the haze to fall with a pallid orange glow upon the rushes and cycads of the swamps and the red-barked wide-branched ginkgos and cypress along the shorelines. The upland trees, conifers similar to pines, firs, and cedars of earth, cast faint double shadows across glades and meadows filled with plants in blossom, whose colored brilliance was a sharp contrast to the soft crepuscular light.

Dawn mists rose from field and fen as the suns warmed the air. The mists oozed away through the trees and the black, broken outcroppings of lava, to mingle with the hazy air that bore faint subliminal odors of sulfur compounds and the dead, burned scents of molten rock and ash. The smoke from a thousand volcanos and a million fumaroles supplied new odors to replace those destroyed by the lush vegetation. It was a world of conflict, a raw, young, vital, volcanic world teeming with plants in furious competitive growth.

The plant growth was matched by an equal abundance of animals. There were amphibians, reptiles, mammals, and saurians. There were huge flying reptilian forms that rode the air currents, their long-snouted, sharp-toothed, counterbalanced heads jutting like pickaxes from the vast spread of their wings. They circled and zigzagged in soaring flight over the jungles, the meadows, the rocky cliffs, and waters of the marshes, their eyes alert for prey upon the surface of the world below.

Saurian forms were dominant on land, in water,

and in air. In general, the aquatic creatures fell into two groups, a wholelike beast with a crocodilian snout, and a larger four-flippered form with a long snakelike neck and a small, viciously armed head that terminated in a beak. The marsh dwellers were also of two general shapes, a bipedal form that looked much like a duckbilled, web-footed kangaroo, and a quadruped that moved about in the shallow waters on four enormously thick, short legs, its barrel body set between a tiny head on a long, flexible neck and a long whiplike tail that tapered from a thick, muscular root.

The land saurians were also bipedal and quadrupedal. Here, however, there was a difference. The bipedal forms were mainly predators, ugly, active beasts with tooth-filled jaws that nearly split their heads in half. They ranged in size from tiny feathered creatures with long, winglike anterior limbs modified for grasping to huge lumbering titans some ten or twelve meters long. The quadrupeds, almost without exception, were herbivores and the larger ones were armed with horns and clothed in defensive armor of plates, scales, and shields of bone or horn. The smaller ones had long muscular legs and could move with considerable speed.

There were also mammals and therapsids, but these, although diverse and numerous, and similarly divided into predators and prey, were small and relatively inconsequential.

In the waters, life swarmed. There were fish and amphibians. There were things that were not quite fish and not quite amphibian. There were the dominant saurians and even a few mammalian forms. There were squid and tentacled shellfish, clams, oysters, and a profusion of snails. The surface waters were alive with tiny crustaceans swimming through thickets of aquatic grasses and kelp. Great islands of organic matter floated on the brackish seas and everywhere there was life, life, life—flying life, swimming life, crawling life, running life, climbing life, burrowing life, all following the instinctual paths that nature had designed for them.

And interspersed among the larger forms were insects and arthropods ranging from dragon flies with half-meter wingspans to tiny things invisible to the naked eye. In point of numbers, at least, they were the largest group upon this fecund world.

There was one omission in the roster. There were no birds. And there was one oddity: there were virtually no juvenile saurians.

A huge, blue-skinned marsh dweller, considerably larger than his fellows, moved laboriously through the mud flats, his weight supported by the mud pressing against his enormous belly. His four pillarlike legs churned slowly, propelling the massive body toward deeper water. The tide was out and he had become much too landborne and too exposed for comfort.

He was hot and was having trouble passing off the heat that his huge body absorbed from the suns. Moreover, he was hungry. Driven by the two needs, he slowly pushed on toward deeper and cooler waters. His head, minuscule in contrast to the enormous bulk of body, swung back and forth on his flexible neck, the sulfur-colored eyes a brilliant contrast to the cobalt skin. He opened his mouth and plunged it below the surface, emerging with a greenish mass of vegetation, which he chewed and swallowed as he plodded out to sea.

Then—suddenly—he stopped. His head lifted and the bright eyes looked skyward. Food and coolness were forgotten for the moment, for to the tiny brain, scarcely as large as a rabbit's, came a primary sensation of danger! It was a sensation the giant hadn't felt for centuries.

Something arced across the sky above the sulfuric haze. The harsh, blue white light preceding it cut an angry path through the air to herald its approach—and as it passed, a thunderclap of sonic boom and screech of riven air followed. It shone brighter than the twin suns, and its passage was marked by swarms of terrified running, swimming, climbing, and flying life. The flying reptiles whirled and tumbled as their delicate sensory apparatus was disrupted by the sonic boom. But the light passed and the activity died, and for a while the predators fed on the disturbed and frightened prey.

The long-necked saurian looked out to sea. He saw that the water had changed and was now coming back across the marshes. He lowered his head and began to feed, confident that in a few moments, as he reckoned them, he would be submerged and cool again. He looked briefly at another of his kind, a smaller, younger, female. No pulses stirred the giant. The season was near, but not yet. All was peaceful. All was as it had been before.

The giant was wrong.

Man—the ultimate predator—had come to this world. This time he had come to explore and classify and name, but there would be a next time. . . .

CHAPTER 1

The *J-17* orbited the planet just outside the Van Allen bands and the atmospheric shell. Inside the ship, part of the crew were busy taking starsights and coordinating navigational data with old charts and tables made by the exploration mission some twenty subjective years before. The remainder were analyzing the planet below.

This was the second visit to this world. The first was an exploratory party that had landed twenty years earlier to investigate planets with Earthlike environments. Benton Dakka, who captained one of the survey ships, had, with his legendary modesty, named most of his discoveries after himself. Since the names were temporary and would be changed by the nomenclature commission, it made no difference—and possibly one of the ten worlds called Dakka that he had discovered would be named after him, which would give him an immortality that most of his contemporaries didn't think he deserved. This world was Dakka VII.

Commander Gene Bishop, skipper of the space freighter *J-17*, couldn't recall exactly when Benton Dakka had landed on the surface of this planet, seventh in his chain of self-named worlds. And it didn't matter to him, for he cared little about such history; his interests lay with his duties—surface conditions, periods of rotation, and landing areas. But he did remember learning of Dakka VII during the first month of an extraterrestrial biology course at Stanford, before he went to prep for space command at academy.

Dakka VII, he recalled, was similar to Earth

as it had been in the Mesozoic era. His Stanford professor had been delighted with the data Benton Dakka had brought back; and Bishop puzzled at the man's interest, since it was already axiomatic that Earthlike environments produced Earthlike ecologies. It wasn't until later, until this voyage in fact, that he'd realized Dr. David Grimsby had been thinking about Dakka VII as a world with potential for colonization.

Grimsby was the scientific director of this mission, and he and his wife, Dian, were the VIP civilians for whom the *J-17* had crossed parsecs of interstellar space. Grimsby had been the last person Bishop would have expected to see aboard his ship, but the professor, like Bishop, had come up in the world and was now an authority on the newly discovered planets.

Bishop had commanded spacecraft for nearly a decade now and was considered one of the best men in the United States Space Fleet. He had been bossing freighters in the government service since his second command, and the *J-17* was the latest in a series of ships that had gotten progressively larger, faster, and more sophisticated.

Those picked for his crews considered themselves lucky, for Bishop had the much-envied reputation of never losing a crew member to disease or accident, only three people had ever died while serving under him: one woman executed for crimes on Alborea and two men kidnapped by the predatory humanoid females on Lesorge. Neither could be called Bishop's fault.

His reputation for luck—and it was true that commanders needed their share of it—grew so large that some claimed his first and middle initials (G. A., for Gene Arthur) stood for Guardian Angel. Bishop, naturally, was proud of the confidence his crews had in him and did his best to keep that confidence, as well as the reputation that had fostered it, intact.

He stood in front of the center viewscreen now, a blue-eyed, ruddy-faced, yellow-haired Viking of the New School. A thousand years earlier he would have been the same, except that the school would have been different, and he would have worn his hair long and in braids. A big, wide, muscular man, harsh of voice and quick of movement, there was violence in him, but it seldom surfaced. He was an obvious leader—that much had been recognized all through his training—well grounded in space technology and accustomed to the responsibilities of command.

The crew, except for Pilot Officer Jeffrey Chalfin and Second Astrogator Cassandra Wecklos, thought he was God Almighty, and Bishop did little to discourage such thought. In fact he took pride in it, and it smoothed out situations which under another commander might have become somewhat ugly. Jeff, however, considered him a friend, and what Cassandra thought was impossible to tell. By long-standing custom, the skipper of a space bucket rated a mistress, and Cassandra filled that role as well as she filled the responsibilities of second astrogator: in an exceptionally competent manner.

Chalfin was at the controls. He had known Bishop for nearly a decade and had managed to like him for most of that time. His leathery face squeezed out a thin smile as he watched his skipper check the landing programs. There was no resentment in the grin. With his last-minute checks old G. A. was simply living up to his nickname.

"Okay Jeff," Bishop said, looking up from the program, "take her down."

Chalfin nodded, checked his coordinates, and put the *J-17* into a standard orbital approach. As the ship slipped into the approach corridor, he turned on the landing computer and followed the approach procedures on the manual keyboard as the computer executed the program.

The ship rotated on its gyros until it was running stern-first down the corridor. Flame bloomed from the main drive as the speed was killed and gravity took charge. From there on, it was routine. The ship came down, balanced on its jets, and sank softly to a clean landing on a rocky outcropping at the edge of a gently sloping meadow. Nearby flowed a fair-sized river.

Drs. Dian and David Grimsby came into the control room as soon as the landing was stabilized and the jets turned off. They seemed a perfect team, both in their late forties or early fifties, and at the height of their mental powers. It was, however, difficult to determine precisely how old they might be, since there were thousands of aids to simulate and stimulate youth in Earth's pharmacopoeia. Bishop had guessed early fifties at the beginning of the voyage but had since decided it didn't really make much difference.

The pair had a prestigious reputation as vertebrate paleontologists, and mutual interest, mutual respect and mutual levels of intelligence all combined to make their marriage work in an age when very few did. Bishop had envied them—slightly—since the first and knew that if he ever married, it would be to secure a relationship such as the Grimsbys had. As skipper of a J-class space freighter, he had little opportunity to pursue marriage, but he decided that after this trip—hopefully his last—he would give the idea a bit more consideration. There was little doubt, that this was his last trip, for a spacer, at age thirty, was considered ready for retirement. Since he had no leanings whatever toward administration, he was going to phase out and go on the beach. Then, perhaps, a wife.

Even though he did envy the Grimsbys, he knew the regulations against marriage for personnel were strict and probably necessary. He had never even thought of questioning the regulations. Besides, there were the usual outlets for the human libido.

Bishop forced his mind back to the Grimsbys. They were representatives of both the Marshal Museum Exploratory Foundation, which had chartered this mission, and the Bureau of Parks, which had sponsored it. Their instructions had been to find and bring back dinosaurs.

"Grimsbys," Bishop started, "I've got a lizard on the starboard screen. Like to see it?"

There was no need for an answer as David and Dian turned toward the screen; their smiles of expectancy replied suitably. As they stood, staring at the ten meters of bipedal toothy horror framed in the center of the starboard viewscreen, the smiles were replaced by the cold, hard interest typical of scientific types. The biped shown on the viewscreen was moving through the tall grass of the meadow outside, stopping occasionally to bend over and pluck a small animal from the grass, carrying the helpless prey to its lipless jaws before biting once, swallowing, and resuming its search for other tidbits.

"About the size of a dog," David Grimsby mused aloud, "beagle-sized or so. Must take a lot of them to keep that fellow full."

Dian shivered, uncharacteristically for one in her professional capacity. "I've never liked carnivores. They're necessary, I suppose, but—"

"They keep the population in balance, that's for sure," David interrupted her, smiling at her momentary shiver. Then, "Look! There! He's got another one. Look at that! They don't even struggle; no resistance at all."

"Probably frozen with fear," Dian said. "I bloody well would be."

David chuckled without looking at his wife. His dark eyes remained on the screen; a wide grin planted itself on his face. Dian, looking at him, was reminded of nothing so much as a little boy grabbing and opening the first present he'd found beneath the traditional glassite Christmas tree.

"Astounding!" David mumbled with enthusiasm, his analytical mind clicking facts into place as he watched the creature on the viewscreen. "A saurian, and from all appearances related to *Allosaurus*, don't you think, Dian?"

"Uh-huh. His relatives aside, imagine his appetite! That's the fourth dog-creature he's eaten, and he doesn't show any signs of filling up!"

"Probably hides in some dark spot to digest," Bishop interjected.

David ran his fingers through his shock of unruly brown hair. "Gene," he said with a touch of awe in his voice, his head moving slowly from side to side, "you'll probably never have the feeling I have right now."

Undoubtedly correct, Bishop decided. The scientist's eyes had yet to leave the image of the bird-footed horror on the viewscreen, and his expression echoed joy at having found such specimens and witnessing them in their natural habitat.

"I don't doubt it a bit," Bishop answered. Then, as an unsettling thought occurred to him, he asked, "You don't mean to take that thing back, do you?"

David chuckled at the barely noticeable tinge of fear in Bishop's voice. "No, only its eggs. We'll hatch them at the foundation. Mind you, it would be nice to have a living Allosaurus, but—"

"I'd rather have a Zabriskan fontema," Bishop interrupted. "They're just as stupid as that thing, but at least they're cute . . . which is more than I can say for your *Allosaurus!*"

Bishop's mention of the Zabriskan fontema was an unintended reminder to the others present that he had seen a great deal in his short subjective life. He had visited the planet the French had discovered, Noveau Afrique, that resembled Africa when that continent still contained animal life. And there was the planet with the islands not unlike the Galapagos of Earth where big marine lizards basked in the sun. They were similar to Earthly iguanas—except, of course, for the pineal eye, which was still functional. And there was the mentioned Zabriska, and a hundred more.

Jeff Chalfin, who had been listening, cut into the conversation. "You're getting a little bland, skipper . . . probably been in space too long." He was ribbing now. "What you need is a nice long rest and retirement pay."

"Don't rush me," Bishop told him.

Dian Grimsby smiled. "You've seen more than we ever will," she said, "so that's probably why you don't feel the excitement a couple of old fossil hunters like David and I—"

"You mean old fossils," David interrupted, smiling, his eyes still on the viewscreen.

". . . a couple of old fossil *hunters* like David and I do," Dian repeated, finishing her statement without further interruption. "Because we've been trying to piece together Earth's entire prehistory from incomplete fragments of bone for years, this moment is sheer ecstasy to us!"

"This is our first opportunity—the first any paleontologist has ever had, for that matter— to observe living dinosaurs," David explained, touches of joy and wonder mingled together in his voice. "And it doesn't matter that these saurians aren't quite the same as those that ruled our Mesozoic; they're close enough."

Bishop didn't need to be a paleontologist to understand the jubilation of the Grimsbys. By the year 2149, when the *J-17* left Earth for Dakka VII, virtually all Earth's animal life had become extinct or was housed in zoos. Perhaps because man was the dominant life form, animal extinction had been inevitable. Oh, the domesticated animals—the horses, the ever-faithful dogs, the ever-faithless cats, rabbits, guinea pigs, mice and countless species of tropical fish—were still doing well under the pampering and care of their masters and owners, but the wild terrestrial animals, the beasts of the forests, hills and jungles, were gone. The only exceptions were those few that persisted in tightly closed and vigilantly patrolled wilderness areas. Wildlife was a fading memory, now, as unreal as the legendary dinosaurs. There were still birds and fish, but the animals, the beautiful, graceful, free animals were gone.

So Bishop didn't have to be an analytical scientist to appreciate the small-brained predator on the viewscreen as it stalked a bloody path across the meadow. Bishop had seen the faces of children and adults alike as they crowded and pushed through such famous wildlife parks as Africa-World and Asia-World to observe alien fauna that were similar to long-extinct Earth species. They could imagine what it had once been like on their own world, and it brought nostalgia and a conviction that if men had another chance, they'd do better the second time around. No one was too concerned with accuracy to complain that the "lions" of Africa-World had tiger stripes, or that "elephants" of Asia-World had two sets of tusks. In a world starved of animals, a little imagination and a smidgeon of acceptance worked wonders.

And now, there were dinosaurs. Upon completion of this mission there would be Dino-World, the latest wildlife park. The *J-17* would transport fauna and flora to grace the newest and greatest of tourist attractions, and it was the Grimsbys' assignment to select and secure the dinosaur eggs for incubation back on Earth.

When the mission was accomplished Bishop would be promoted to curator (how he detested that title!) of Dino-World. Thirty-one was wash-up age for ship commanders and the space service took care of its retired personnel. He could at last relax from the time-devouring flights that had claimed his last ten subjective (nearly fifty objective) years. Once again, Bishop would call the Earth, home. He could marry and enjoy life with a woman who knew how to give and share rather than one like Cassandra who took and enjoyed. Yet this was unkind of him, he realized, for he took and enjoyed. Actually they took from each other in acts that were a kind of mutual theft.

Bishop fantasized a little as he waited for the laboratory reports on the livability of this world. Dakka had said it was three-plus, which meant that no space suits or protective devices were needed, but Bishop trusted no lab but his own. If the index were below three-minus he didn't want his people out in it without protection. But that wasn't the subject on his mind. He was daydreaming of a luxury office, with simulated wood furniture and thick synthewool carpets, completely equipped with the latest computers and a few sleek and attractive girls to run them. He dreamed of exotic food and drink, of soft lights and music, of civilization and lovely women. . . .

Chalfin shattered the dream. "We're ready to open up, sir," the pilot said. "Lab reports the index is just under four. It's as near Earth as you can get. A little too much sulfur, a little too much water vapor, but nothing harmful. Shorts and insect repellent! Hallelujah!"

Jeff Chalfin and Cassandra Wecklos were among the six crew members who accompanied David and Dian Grimsby and Gene Bishop outside the *J-17*. They stood approximately thirty meters from the freighter and examined this lush paradise. Paradise? Bishop wondered. Certainly it was no Eden for the doglike animals the saurian had eaten. Where *was* that saurian? Moved off to digest? He didn't know, but at any rate, it wasn't in sight. He stretched and savoured the fresh air and physical freedom, satisfied that this planet had a breathable atmosphere and a bearable temperature.

Swarms of insects circled at respectful distances from the repellent-coated crew members, causing Bishop to ask Cassandra, "Think they'd bite if we didn't have the repellent?"

She rubbed her bare arms. "Probably," she shrugged, "but I don't think I'll make any experiments to find out for sure. Besides, I'm not too nuts about getting in and out of those lousy protection suits; the repellent fits fine."

Bishop chuckled.

Neither of the Grimsbys were interested in the banter. Their attention was riveted on the beauties of Dakka VII; where sharply etched mountains rose from the misty plain; where distant volcanos belched smoke and ash to partially obscure the twin suns; where lush green jungle and incredibly lovely flowers blended into a tapestry of kaleidoscopic color.

Beautiful as it was, however, the Grimsbys were

not observing the terrain and the flora with the intensity of interest they observed the animals.

"Plesiosaurus!" David exclaimed in wonder, noticing the intruders suddenly.

Coming toward them from the direction of the river was a group of five saurians.

"Welcoming committee!" Bishop snapped. "Draw and charge blasters! Load rifles!"

As the monsters approached the landing party, the men checked their weapons and moved back to the entrance of the spaceship.

The group of saurians was an odd assortment: a duckbill, a mid-sized marsh grazer Bishop thought of as a *Brontosaurus*, a Ceratopsia—the lizard equivalent of a rhinoceros, and two bipedal frog-faced toothy horrors even larger than the *Allosaurus* Bishop's people had seen on the monitor screen.

Bishop drew his blaster and checked the charge, satisfied to find it fully loaded. He nodded absently to himself and transferred his attention to the saurians, which had stopped approximately fifty meters away to observe the humans.

"They . . . they're all wrong," Dian Grimsby said, the immediacy of the danger overruled by her professional interest. "Three of them are herbivores."

"So what?" Bishop asked. "They're all bloody dinosaurs, aren't they?"

Of that, of course, there was no doubt; any schoolchild could have determined that. In a strange way he couldn't quite comprehend, Bishop saw the group as a committee.

"Yes, they are," Dian said slowly, "but their

behavior is wrong. Carnosaurs and herbivores shouldn't be standing side by side."

"I don't think Dino-World visitors will complain," David said, choosing to ignore the contradictions before him as he remembered his official capacity on this journey. "They're impressive, and they look ferocious."

"They may be as ferocious as they *look*," Bishop said with a cautious edge to his voice. "I don't want to be without a line of retreat, so keep your eyes open."

"Come off it, skipper," Chalfin said, chuckling. "Those overgrown lizards are as uncertain as we are. There's no sign of trouble."

"So far," Bishop added. He looked at the crew, satisfied to see them armed and alert as he had ordered. Even Cassandra looked efficient with a blaster in hand. Perhaps Chalfin was right, Bishop reflected, but he wasn't taking any chances. He didn't relish the thought of opening fire on the saurians, but if he had to, he wouldn't hesitate. Especially since the size of the air lock would prevent the entire group from entering the ship in a single group if the beasts did charge.

"Dian and Cassandra, get into the ship," Bishop ordered, his decision made, cautious and careful as always. "You too, David. The rest of you set for maximum charge, minimum aperture. If you have to fire, aim for their heads, the leader first. In any case, don't fire until I give the word. That's an order!"

Dian and David Grimsby, along with Cassandra Wecklos, had started toward the air lock, moving backwards, their eyes still on the group of saurians.

"Leapin' lizards," Chalfin said softly, to no one in particular.

Someone laughed.

There had been a resurrection of Little Orphan Annie cartoons on video just before they'd left Earth, and the Moppet's favorite expression had been on everyone's lips, which was not surprising, considering the nature of the mission.

"Shut up!" Bishop ordered, not finding the expression particularly amusing in light of their present circumstances.

Then, almost as if attracted by Bishop's voice, one of the saurians moved. Ponderously, yet with an odd grace, the others followed, toward Bishop and his command.

CHAPTER 2

As suddenly as they had started, the five dinosaurs stopped and continued to stare at the humans, who continued to stare back, nervous, uncertain.

"If they move toward us again," Bishop murmured, "we'll start firing. One warning blast, then we get serious."

There was a scraping noise behind them, and Cassandra's voice followed it almost immediately "We've got a semiportable set up in the air lock It'll stop them with no trouble."

"Good, good," Bishop said. "Okay, stay loose. And don't fire unless I give the word."

The dinosaurs, however, seemed ready to continue standing and observing, making no more moves toward the ship. Which was fine as far as the humans were concerned, for it gave them an excellent chance to study the planet's dominant life forms.

Generally, the saurians fitted the rough classification Dian and David had described to the crew during the voyage from Earth, prime examples of the four-legged and bipedal types.

Two of the five were carnivores, bipedal, sharp toothed members of a suborder similar to Theropoda, according to the Grimsbys. Although the identification was easy, these were not simply theropods, but carnosaurs—the huge predators of *Allosaurus* and *Tyrannosaurus* variety, towering bipedal monsters with small forelimbs and gigantic, froglike heads weaponed with long, double edged teeth. The only apparent differences between the reconstructions of Earth's carnosaurs and these gaudy, yellow-bellied monsters were the bony protuberances protecting each yellow eye of the Dakkan lizards and the longer forelimbs, each of which ended with five digits as opposed to the two or three that the Earthly species possessed. The color was unexpected, but so were the pale green and white stripes on the back of the marsh grazer, and the gaudy yellow, red and orange masks of the horned lizard. It was a living tank— virtually identical to an Earthly styracosaur except for the twin-lipped orange horn that surmounted the yellow-beaked snout and the thick armor plating along its purple back. There was also a smooth-skinned yellow duckbill of the *Trachodon* type, looking less formidable than Donald Duck!

The *Brontosaurus*, as it would inevitably be called at Dino-World, lowered its head close to the ground and looked up at the ship with sulfur-yellow eyes. When the creature shifted its gaze to Bishop, the commander shivered despite the tropical temperature. If he hadn't known that dinosaurs were virtually brainless and that some had more nerve tissue in their rumps than their heads, he would have sworn that the creature was analyzing him.

"Absolutely amazing," Dian Grimsby's hushed voice came from above and behind.

Bishop risked a quick look, seeing the two paleontologists standing close together in the air lock, beside the semiportable. At a glance, he could tell they too were surprised at the way these animals stood and stared. Bishop's crew, following orders, were motionless and alert. Cassandra, intelligently enough, was behind the semiportable, ready to commence operation.

"Well, Commander," Dian Grimsby started as the saurians stood and seemed to grumble at each other, "what happens now?"

"I don't know," Bishop admitted, not sure whether he should order everyone back inside the ship or not. "But we'll probably find out in a minute. Look at 'em . . . looks like they're having a conference."

Indeed, stupid and savage as they appeared, the saurians seemed to be intelligently reflecting upon the matter at hand. The concept seemed silly to Bishop, but there they were.

"It's all wrong," Dian persisted from the air lock. "There are two carnosaurs we'll call them allosaurs to make it simple—but they're not acting like carnosaurs."

Each of the flesh-eaters stood balanced upon its muscular hind legs, its taloned feet digging into the moist soil, and its birdlike body horizontal to the ground, counterweighted by a huge head and a heavy tail.

"I think," Chalfin started slowly, but confidently, "that if they were going to attack us, they'd'a done it by now."

"I wish I could agree," Dian called out to him, "but carnosaurs have big bellies and big appetites. When they're not sleeping, they're hungry. When they're not hungry, they sleep. I don't understand why they're not attacking, but be careful; they still might."

"If they're always hungry," Bishop mused, loudly enough that all heard him, "why don't they take a leg or two off that duckbill? They should at least be hassling the thing . . . giving it a rough time of some description, if what you say is true."

Bishop was still speaking when the five dinosaurs ceased swaying gently from side to side on their muscular legs, and turned their attention from the spacecraft and the humans who stood around it, to each other. Carnosaur Number One, as Bishop had mentally christened the beast, suddenly moved backwards, crushing vegetation beneath its enormous claws, its tail slicing through the air behind it. Its jaws clomped shut several times, barely missing the spine of the duckbilled reptile. The duckbill ran swiftly toward the river, suddenly pursued by the slower predator.

"Get into the ship!" Bishop barked. "Move it! They might turn on us!"

Chalfin and the crew backed quickly toward the air lock. The Grimsbys disappeared, although Dian had to tug at her husband's arm before he budged, so intent was he on his observation of the one-moment-peaceful/next-moment-savage saurians. Bishop stood with the gunner of the semiportable as the air lock doors closed, and the last thing he saw was the *Brontosaurus* cautiously moving its neck beyond biting range of Carnosaur Number Two, who seemed to be uncertain as to the most efficient method of decapitating his enemy.

Bishop's attention went immediately to the air lock viewscreen, and he saw the styracosaur already ambling off toward the plain as the *Brontosaurus* slowly moved toward the river where the first meat-eater had finally turned back. Its clawed feet, unlike the duckbill's webbed ones, had no flotation, and it floundered miserably. Its prey had already vanished into the rushes, and both flesh-eaters now confronted the marsh grazer.

Bishop watched the imminent confrontation, vaguely aware of a tingling excitement racing up and down his spine. "This is it," he murmured to the gunner, preparing himself for the battle that should have been in progress from the very beginning.

But this wasn't it, Bishop saw a few seconds later. The brontosaur, with almost ludicrous ease, avoided the suddenly clumsy carnivores and escaped into the water with only a couple of spines missing from its back plates, not even enough to cause it any noticeable pain.

"Aw, geez," the gunner beside Bishop suddenly lamented. "I was expectin' somethin' fierce. If that's all they do. . . ."

He let his voice trail off, but Bishop wanted to hear a bit more. The gunner's words had started him thinking. "What do you mean?" he asked.

"Well, cripes, don't you remember all the illustrations they've been using to advertise this new park? Pictures showing dinosaurs fighting to the death, ripping each other apart. Tyrannosaurs eating brontosaurs . . . survival of the fittest and the strongest and the most savage. That's all people have been hearin' about, and that's what they'll probably expect at Dino-World."

"I see what you mean," Bishop said slowly. "If what we saw was any indication, the people back on Earth are going to be a little disappointed, because these babies sure aren't the savages they're supposed to be. People will be asking for their money back, sure thing."

Bishop watched the air lock screen as the two carnosaurs stood on the riverbank and observed the brontosaur as it moved deeper into the water. After snapping at each other in what seemed like futility—although no actual blows or bites were seen by Bishop—they stalked off in opposite directions, in search of smaller and easier game. Perhaps the doglike creatures.

Bishop left the air lock, returning to the control room where everyone had been watching the "battle" on the viewscreen.

"Wasn't much of a battle, was it Gene?" Cassandra asked him.

Jeff Chalfin chuckled, without waiting for Bishop to reply. "It was a dud, Cass. Even pro wrestlers put up a better show than that!"

CHAPTER 3

"So far," Dian said, "we haven't seen any vast number of dinosaurs, though we have seen representatives of six suborders that correspond to those of Earth. Remember, we've been commissioned by the foundation to bring back the fertile eggs of all six."

She sounded like a professor, Bishop thought. She couldn't help it; it probably was an occupational disease.

"On Earth and under the order Saurischia," she said, "we had only two: Theropoda, the flesh-eaters, and Sauropoda, those long-necked behemoths exemplified by the incorrectly named *Brontosaurus*. The order Ornithischia, however, gives us four suborders: Ornithopoda, including iguanodonts and duckbills; Stegosauria, the plated dinosaurs, and Ankylosauria, the armored dinosaurs; and Ceratopsia, the ones with shields protecting their necks and horns on their noses and above their eyes."

"We want representatives of each suborder," interjected David Grimsby. "Having specimens will enhance the realism of Dino-World. And it'd be nice to get a number of the smaller varieties of saurians, reptiles, and therapsids. We can fill out the mammals with excess we have on hand in the other parks."

Bishop grinned, "You certainly want to give the dinosaur buffs their money's worth."

"Exactly," said Dian. "But more important than that, having all six suborders represented will give us the opportunity to study their habits and observe how they interact."

"I see," Bishop said, "but while you're studying those lizards, they may also be studying you."

"That's ridiculous," David said.

"I'm not so sure," said Bishop. "I can't forget the way that *Brontosaurus* looked at us and at the ship. I felt as if I were a guinea pig under observation!"

Bishop waited for a reply but received none. "All right," he said, "we'll bring back the eggs of all six groups. But where do we begin our alien egg hunt? If I remember correctly from my youthful readings about dinosaurs, the big lizards weren't gregarious or family-oriented. They were just supposed to lay their eggs in a kind of nest in the sand, then abandon them to the heat of the sun, which hopefully would do the rest. If you ask me, that makes a hell of a lot of territory to cover, just for a few dozen eggs."

There was a knowing smile on David Grimsby's face. "You seem to have remembered a lot from your boyhood readings, Gene," he said.

"We even have some of those nests," added Dian, "thanks to the *Protoceratops* discoveries in the Gobi Desert by Roy Chapman Andrews back in the twentieth century."

"But we're not on Earth now," said Bishop. "And we still don't know how to cover all that territory out there to find a few eggs."

"Don't you remember what Benton Dakka said about this world in his published reports?"

Bishop remembered little about the Dakka reports. Whatever passages involved dinosaur eggs were long forgotten. He did, however, recall seeing a nest of eggs on display in the hall of vertebrate paleontology on the second floor of the Marshal Natural History Museum, along with the skeleton of the animal that laid them. *Protoceratops andrewsi* was its name. He remembered that clearly.

"Dakka reported," said Dian, "that he saw the reptiles of this planet laying their eggs. But unlike *Protoceratops* and her contemporaries, Dakka's dinosaurs are motivated by some inner drive that causes them to congregate in a single location to lay them."

"How nice," Bishop said. "It reminds me of those old stories about the Elephants' Graveyard, only in reverse."

"Benton Dakka was on this planet for a full month, Earth time," said David. "And he was able to learn where the reptiles deposited their eggs."

"Where?" Bishop asked.

"The riverbanks," David informed him, indicating the river that wound among the forest growth. The growth was gradually disappearing in the darkness of encroaching evening.

"When?" Bishop wanted to know.

"Right now," Dian told him. "This mission was planned to coincide with the dinosaur laying season, and according to calculations by the Marshal Museum computers, the laying season will continue for another three weeks."

"Then we've got plenty of time," Bishop said, nodding, "and there's no big rush."

"And it shouldn't be too difficult to go down the river and watch for nests," Dian mused.

"They're too big to camouflage places they've visited and the results of those visits."

Bishop looked at the mountain peaks, almost regal in the distance, seeing the twin suns sinking slowly toward them. Soon it would be night. "Plenty of time," he murmured softly.

"We'd like to get started soon, though," Dian said, as shadows continued to darken the land. "We've been waiting a heckuva long time for this chance."

Bishop understood completely. "Fine," he told her, looking over to David Grimsby. "We'll get started tomorrow."

Dian smiled.

CHAPTER 4

Night was descending rapidly upon the jungle. Only a trace of yellow light pierced the upper canopy, while beneath the lower canopy, it was already dark. Rust-colored vines joined one tree to the next and disappeared into shadows, lost in the almost ominous blackness. The sounds of night insects—what there were of them—echoed and reechoed, at first only a few, then a rising crescendo till the jungle came alive with the sounds. Occasionally, the insects ceased their mindless babble, and there was complete silence; but within a few moments after the final echo had died, they invariably started again.

Waning light gleamed on the surface of the ponds, lakes and marshes, each green with algae and thick with microscopic animal life. Hundreds of billions of flying insects buzzed in hordes over the scummy water, their own dull droning adding to the cacophony of night.

Nights were not safe on Dakka VII, and occasionally the tromping sounds of a creature, heard but not seen, echoed. This clomping caused even the insects to cease the mindless screeching.

It would take exceptional eyes to pierce the darkness of night in the jungle, and only a life form used to the black could hope to survive for any length of time. Such an exceptional pair of eyes belonged to the woman who waited in the lower canopy of the jungle growth, crouched in the V of a branching tree trunk, a spear held firmly in one hand, while the other clutched the red—black under nighttime—bark of the tree.

Her name was Leea, and in the treetops above, her mate lined their sleeping platform with new leaves that would serve as their nest for the night. Konu did not put a great deal of effort into his work, nor did he take much pride in his construction—although he was careful to build the nest in more than haphazard security fashion—for like all their recent resting places, this nest was temporary, providing a brief respite in their flight from the *reeka*. It could not even be called a home, for those who fled the reeka had no home. Life was a constant flight, from cave to cave, from tree to tree, from plain to mountain; never could they stop for too long in one place. To do so was to be discovered by the reeka, and to be discovered by the reeka was to die.

They had been fleeing for some time now, ever since a reeka had come to the caves of their tribe and fallen into a pit constructed by Konu, a pit fitted with thick, sharply pointed stakes at the bottom. The reeka had impaled itself from belly to back and had died a horrible, shrieking death.

Konu was a hero because of his pit and the dead reeka; and to him went the honor of removing the teeth of the reeka, fashioning them into a necklace for his mate to wear. No other woman in the tribe had a necklace such as that which Leea wore proudly around her neck, and the envy directed toward her was intense.

But with the supreme honor of slaying a reeka came responsibility, almost a penalty. If no additional reeka came to the caves of the tribe, all would be well. But if more reeka should appear, then Konu and Leea must run and decoy the feared horrors away from the remainder of the tribe. And there was little chance of the reeka not coming, for never had they failed to come, not even in the most heroic of legends. So even though Konu was a hero and his woman respected for the privilege of bedding a hero, he was also doomed, and it was only a matter of time . . . for both of them. The tender farewell ceremony had been held—when the tribe gathered in the deepest cave by the Place of Water to wish them both as much luck as the gods would bestow—and then had come the time of waiting.

And then the reeka.

Not as many as in the old days, but enough to make their flight a matter of necessity if the tribe were to survive. So run they did, trailing bags of scent to attract the reeka and lure them away from the caves. The beasts followed in the manner of their kind, never realizing they had been tricked, for the reeka obeyed laws and whims that were not those of men.

Leea shivered, wishing that Konu would hurry with the nest, for it was getting cold in the V where she waited. Soon, as the darkness became blacker, not even her exceptional eyes would be able to pierce the night, and in these reeka-infested regions one needed every advantage, all the senses available to escape the creatures.

She stretched, easing her cramped muscles, and wished for a robe of warm varden fur to shield her from the chill. A leather breechclout wasn't much protection; Konu's warmth and the leaves of the nest would be much better.

She wrapped her arms around her torso, waiting for her mate's call. It would be soon, she knew, for he loved and desired her, but that did not ease the impatience she felt tightening in her, nor did it drive away the cold that made her shiver.

To make the time pass quickly, she thought of her beauty, for she possessed much and knew it. The still pools of water reflected the beauty of her face and hair, of her smooth, unblemished skin—pure red with only the faintest tracery of purple veins—whenever she bathed or had occasion to admire herself. Her red skin blended perfectly with the bark of the tree and could not be easily seen. It would be poor protection against a reeka, however, and this knowledge caused her even greater impatience as she looked up to the topmost canopy where her slow mate still worked on the nest. His tardiness would cause him death some day.

She touched the knife in her belt, calling upon its magic to aid her, then whispered to the god in her spear to protect her. And still she waited, unwilling to help, for the making of the nest was a man's job. And, there was some fear, because until the nest was completed, she would be vulnerable; flying reeka were sometimes abroad after the sun had settled below the horizon. She sighed, wishing Konu could be faster, wishing he was less careful and more eager. But Konu's meticulous preparation of a nest that would be safe from the reeka was the result of his many seasons of life—five hands and a thumb of them, one finger for each season—and he had remained alive for so long because of it. Whereas she, having seen less than four hands of seasons, had yet to become careful, cautious, meticulous.

Still he worked, and so she thought of him, remembered the time his wife had been eaten by a reeka, remembered Konu fighting the other males of the tribe for *her* and winning easily. The other men dared not touch her after that.

She heard his voice then and dismissed her thoughts as she climbed up the tree to the nest. Then the noises of night life suddenly ceased, and as its echoes died away, she stopped moving, ears straining for a sound—any sound—that would tell her what was happening.

She was a goodly distance up the tree and clung tightly to it as she saw a movement in the almost total blackness below. Something huge, dark and silent passed ten or twelve meters beneath her. She was thankful that she was above its scent and that her own was faint, for she had bathed that afternoon. If the air would only remain still. . . .

It did and the monster passed by. She shivered, then scrambled up the tree to join Konu in the nest he had prepared. She looked at him with satisfaction, even though he was not a handsome man. His beard was too thick, his skin too rough, his body far too scarred for beauty. His white teeth were broken, and a scar twisted his mouth into the cruel smile that never left his lips. Yet he was gentle with her, a brave warrior and an expert hunter; he had done something that no one else in the tribe had managed—killed a reeka—and no amount of physical beauty would be preferable to that act of heroism. That they were still alive at this moment was a tribute to his skill, and his skill alone.

They touched each other's temples with their fingers and thought of love. The reeka could not understand love; it was something the creatures had never known. Anger, they knew, and fear, and hunger and hate, but unlike the other animals of the land they knew neither love nor joy. And thus, thoughts of love confused them, made the thinkers of such thoughts safe for a time.

She untied her loincloth and came into Konu's arms, and for a while they were secure in the nest. In the tired peace that followed, they rested. And for a while their dreams were pleasant as they lay side by side, taking warmth and comfort from each other.

Below them, faint in the distance, a reeka roared. The frustrated note was music to their ears. They sighed and slept, dreaming of forever-frustrated reeka on a world where the trees were too high and strong to be torn down and the caves too deep and twisted for the reeka's spells to reach.

There were such places. They had lived in one and the legends told of others, places where men could live and reeka could not. But the other places must be few and far away because in all their wandering they had found none.

SIMULTANEOUSLY they awakened and spoke the words of joy. Their spirits were uplifted as the dawn came forth. They would lie here now till midday drove the reeka to their slumbers.

Noon came and they were again on their way. They moved cautiously, for the jungle was cool and the reeka might awaken. They saw one of the furry, stupid animals; Konu killed it with his spear and tied the carcass to his belt. At least they would eat tonight. She found some roots along the way and washed them in a stream before slipping them into a fold of her loincloth. Leea wished that this jungle would end and that they would find another red tree. It was getting late.

They came to the jungle's edge. Ahead, less than half a kilometer away, stood a grove of red trees. But as they left the jungle to cross the open savannah, a roar of triumph sounded behind them! A reeka!

Leea moaned with terror. There was no place to hide, no place to run except toward the red trees. To turn back to the jungle was worse than useless, for the reeka could move faster there than they. Here they had a chance. Instinctively she ran with the long flowing stride of a distance runner. Behind her, panting already, came Konu. She was fast, but for the moment at least, he was faster. He passed her and ran ahead, opening a widening space between them.

And behind them came the reeka. Dian would have identified it as a *Sauropoda* thecodont of the *Spinosaurus* type. To Leea it was walking death. Its limb movements were slow, but its strides were enormous and it kept pace with the fleeing humans. Possibly the two gained a little, but not enough and the trees and safety were still far away.

The beast was the typical flesh-eater, though not the largest of them. Its brown and orange body was less colorful than those of the larger saurians, but just as deadly. A spiny membrane, like the dorsal fin of a fish, ran down its back. Now, in the excitement of hunger and the chase, the fin was erect and gleamed a brilliant orange in the light of the double sun. Saliva dripped in viscid strings from its grinning jaws. The yellow eyes were brilliant in their deep sockets, and the short, sharp nasal horn shone like polished mahogany.

The pair's defenses were reduced to the elemental flight, their last resort. Run, and hopefully outdistance pursuit. Run until muscles ached. Run until each breath was agony. Run until flesh could stand no more, and, if enough distance was put between prey and predator, hide, and stay hidden, quivering, still and silent, hoping that the predator would pass by the fear-filled prey. And so they ran, and behind them came the ponderous footfalls of the saurian's taloned feet.

They reached the red-barked trees; like two squirrels they scrambled up the rough bark of the nearest and into the spreading branches. They did not stop there for they knew the saurian had seen them. The flesh-eaters' eyes were keen. And so they ran along the spreading branches of the middle course, leaping from one branch to another and from tree to tree, separating as they ran. They could rejoin later. Now, they must stay alive.

Leea could do no more. With the last of her strength she climbed into the upper branches of one of the larger trees and crouched into a V-shaped branching. Now she must hide. Now she must think of other things than death and dying. Now she must control her panting breath as the saurian prowled beneath her scanty cover. She was beyond the reach of its jaws and hands, but reeka had other ways of drawing prey from cover, and those were the deadly ones. One could not look upon the beast and live. One closed her eyes and thought good thoughts and hoped. But how to think thoughts of joy and love when that grinning, toothy head poked through the lower courses, snuffling and salivating as it searched with its dreadful seeking eyes for the hidden prey.

She crouched in darkness behind her closed lids and quivered in unreasoning terror as the heavy footfalls came from below. She went limp with relief as they passed, and stiff with terror as they stopped! She could hear something rustling in the branches, but she dared not look. There was a sudden silence. Then again came the rustling and the measured footfalls fading, stopping, and then a scream of triumph and a screech of terror!

Leea's eyes flew open. Fifty meters away the sauropod was circling another tree, its great walking legs moving in measured strides, the horned, grinning head raised in the air, the great jaws half-opened, the bright yellow eyes trying to get a full view of the tiny red figure that circled the trunk in the upper courses of the tree.

Konu! she thought despairingly. But Konu was dead now. The reeka would wait. The reeka was patient when it hunted man. The reeka would call to its blood and its blood would answer. The flying reeka would come, and Konu would be eaten. The reeka pushed against the tree and the branches shook. It bellowed and the sound was answered from beyond the forest. This was no place to be. For a moment she hesitated and then quickly slipped to the ground and ran. She could do nothing for her mate, and were it she who was trapped, he, too, would run. For no one escaped the reeka when the devil's eyes locked on one's own.

The breathing space had restored her strength and she fled silently and swiftly toward the river. There were holes in the bank where she could hide, and perhaps tomorrow she could find a safer place. She felt a stab of pity for Konu. His plight was hopeless, but hers was not much better, for without a man, her chances of survival were reduced to the vanishing point. She would have to find another of her kind and do it quickly if she were to live.

Unlike the jungle there were many obstructions in a forest. At the ground level of jungle, only roots, lianas, and leaf mold filled with fungi and small pale growing things covered the damp thin soil. But in a forest there was underbrush and roots and thorny vines. These hindered the flight of man but did not bother the reeka at all.

Leea was forced to move more slowly than she wished. The suns were sinking. Evening was coming and she had found neither a nesting tree nor a hole in which to hide. Worry slowly turned to fear. The gods were unkind and had turned their faces from her. With growing anxiety she scanned the trees and ground as she moved along a narrow game trail toward the river.

Perhaps, she thought, she should have tried to distract the monster. That way both Konu and she might have escaped. She shook her head. No, that wouldn't have worked. It would have provided two bodies on whom the beast could feed. She hoped that Konu would enter the Spirit World quickly and with little pain. She hoped he would not look into the eyes of the reeka, for then his soul would die with his body.

Leea came at last to the river and gazed at the low flat ground, sighing with frustration as she looked up and down the stream. She needed a bank. Ah! There! Upstream, not far from where she stood was a cutbank carved from the soft volcanic rock. There might be shelter.

There was a crashing in the brush ahead, a frantic scrambling; scarcely a spear cast away Konu broke into the open. His skin was torn and bleeding; his mouth was open, and his breath came in huge pants. His hair was tangled and his face a mask of fear. He looked wildly up and down the river, and then ran in stumbling steps along the direction she had been traveling.

And behind him, crashing through the brush, came the reeka!

Konu! she thought wildly. How had he lived? How had he escaped? It was a miracle, yet it was a miracle she could have done without, for now the reeka was at hand! Quickly she rolled beneath some vine-covered brush, heedless of the thorns that scratched her, as the great claw-footed saurian crashed through the underbrush. The flat, evil horn-nosed head swung quickly from side to side, peering with piercing eyes up and down the river. The dorsal crest, flattened against the backbone, sprang erect and the reeka began to run with undiminished speed after the fleeing man.

The devil! It isn't even tired! Leea thought despairingly. Poor Konu! How had he escaped?

The lizard crashed out of her view, following the man. There were noises in the brush, crashings, snappings, and rustlings as the reeka worked back and forth, searching for its hidden prey. And then suddenly there was silence.

Still hiding within the brush, Leea squirmed forward and saw the sail-backed monster move slowly back from the brushy growth along the riverbank, its fin erect, its tail stiff and lifted off the ground. She knew what had happened, why there was no longer any need for it to pursue its prey. It had found Konu. She tasted bile in her mouth. She wanted to vomit, but she dared not.

With morbid fascination, Leea watched as the monster backed toward her, its horned head facing the direction that Konu had fled. Beyond the head was Konu, moving slowly and submissively as though he had no will of his own. His eyes were staring, wide and glassy. When the reeka stopped, he halted and stared without expression at the head facing him. The great jaws opened. The sharp teeth gleamed briefly as they closed over the staring face. There was a crunching, ripping sound.

Leea closed her eyes. Her stomach heaved, and two tears oozed between her closed lids. For an eternity the reeka fed, but at last it was done. It shook its head and turned toward the river to drink, and Leea came from hiding, circled the grisly relics of her mate, and hurried without a backward glance toward the hoped-for safety of the bank ahead.

She cast a final glance toward the saurian at the river's edge. Its dorsal fin lowered as it drank with greedy gulps. Even at this distance she could hear the rumbling of its gut. Silent and unnoticed, Leea fled from the scene.

As she made her way through the torn brush, her eye caught the shine of polished obsidian. She stopped and picked up Konu's spear. It should properly be buried with him to arm him in the spirit world, but his soul had gone into the eyes of the reeka even as his body had gone into its belly. The spear was hers and she would keep it. She had lost her mate. Later she would mourn him, but now there was no time. She sighed. That was the way of this world. If she lived long enough she might well lose several more. The important thing was that she was alive. Yet how long could she survive when there was no one to bring the protecting thoughts, when there was no one to watch while she slept, when her only protection was a spear?

CHAPTER 5

Cassandra and Bishop made love in his quarters that night. The skipper rated a cabin and privacy; something that the lesser officers and crew didn't have. Cassandra shared her tiny cabin with Sue Madden, the medic. Sue had a sporadic affair going with one of the engineering mates, and she was always glad when Cassandra went to the skipper's cabin. Cassandra liked the relative spaciousness of Bishop's quarters and the luxury of his double bed. Spacing was a hard life, and you had to love it to endure it. And you took every luxury you could get.

Theirs was a professional arrangement, sanctioned by custom, tempered by need, and neither of them really cared that it was not something more. Bishop sighed. It wouldn't be long before this interlude was ended. Cassandra would go back to space; he would be Earthside with the kind of freedom he could never have aboard ship—he wondered idly if he would really enjoy it. After a decade in space, a man gets into certain habits. He sighed contentedly, and slept.

In the morning, Bishop stood in the air lock and looked across the brightening landscape. In a few hours they would be ready to start their search. Meanwhile there was much to do. The hydrofoil jetboat must be taken from the hold and assembled. A survey party must be selected. Arms, food and equipment must be prepared. The materials the Grimsbys needed must be packed. It would be a busy time for everyone.

Returning inside, Bishop joined the Grimsbys and a dozen of his crew. All were breakfasting on the reconstituted rations that, by necessity, were a spaceman's diet. Bishop's soul yearned for steak, but he put the thought aside. Maybe when this was all finished and they were ready to leave, he would try to shoot one of those small dinosaurs that looked oddly like plucked hundred-kilogram chickens; perhaps they could all enjoy a feast of real meat. Dinosaurs were related to birds, so possibly they tasted the same. He recalled a classic story from twentieth-century science fiction that said they did. Now maybe on Earth, he'd have the opportunity to test the predicting power of that ancient author. Asimou? Was that his name?

Meat of any kind was a luxury and the rare occassions he did enjoy steak almost always occurred on some other planet.

The work parties did their assigned tasks, and by midday the boat was assembled, the gear stowed and the search party loaded. The whole affair was conducted under the benign eyes of a pair of brontosaurs, a couple of *Trachodons* and a *Triceratops* that had been attracted by the commotion. The saurians watched with apparent interest as the twenty-second century rubbed elbows with the Mesozoic era.

The search party, except for the Grimsbys, was armed with the powerful blast rifles. Only the semiportable was left behind. These weapons and a boat that could go 70 kilometers per hour would give them a sufficient tactical advantage if any of the larger saurians attacked. As for the smaller ones, the blasters would be more than enough.

"We're ready to go, sir," said Chalfin.

"Well, then, let's get about it," Bishop said. Followed by Chalfin and the others, he stepped into the craft.

The engine caught on the second try and the boat moved out slowly from the shoreline into the mainstream. Chalfin revved the engine to clear the pumps of algal scum, and in a few minutes they were up on the foils and moving down the river at forty kilometers per hour.

The green shoreline sped by as they went through a series of oxbow loops. There was little to see except the brushy banks and jungle. They swept past a narrow spot where the river changed its character and rushed through a rocky narrow cut from volcanic rock. The top of the cutbank was lined with cave mouths, some large enough to shelter a man.

Chalfin pointed to them. "Wonder what's in those caves?" he said.

"Cavemen maybe," Bishop said. "We've got everything else."

Beyond the narrows, the river widened and both sides were bordered by stretches of mudbank interspersed with thick growths of grassy vegetation. A reptile, resembling Earth's *Plesiosaurus*, paddled downstream, its long neck twisted so the tiny head and beaklike snout pointed at the boat. The head was tiny only in a relative sense. Actually the jaws were more than half a meter wide. Presently it sank beneath the water.

Seated in the fore section of the hydrofoil craft, Bishop checked the course and speed and watched for logs, deadheads and other obstructions. Chalfin steered. The Grimsbys scanned the shoreline for evidence of nests, and the two crewmen kept their eyes open for trouble. It was about as good an arrangement as could be devised on short notice, and while Bishop and the crew kept a lookout for the plesiosaur, it didn't make a second appearance. The only fauna present besides the swarms of small insects were a few enormous dragonflies that buzzed across the beaches and a pair of pterodactyl-type reptiles that swung in lazy circles in the sky, looking like bat-winged vultures.

Chalfin maneuvered the hydrofoil along the river and down into the delta region. The boat ran up and down the interlocking waterways until it came to a small lagoon with sandy shores.

"There!" David Grimsby yelled, pointing toward the shoreline on the port side. "Stop!" He staggered to his feet, staggered as Chalfin cut the jets and the ship slid down into the water, then managed to regain his equilibrium.

"Eggs," he said, and he was almost shivering with excitement. He pointed again toward the shoreline. "Dakka was right," he said to no one in particular. "They're laying their eggs."

Five saurians, all armored dinosaurs of a suborder akin to Ankylosauria, were standing on the riverbank. They were oddly tortoiselike, with carapace, plastron, and armored head, legs and tail. All five were large, easily four or five meters in length according to Bishop's mental calculations. Sharp horns on the partly retractable heads gave a ceratopsian touch. The tail, a series of overlapping rings of armor, terminated in a massive ball that bore half a dozen thick, sharp, bony spines.

It was an impressive group, grunting and wheezing comfortably, and taking absolutely no notice of anyone or anything about the immediate vicinity. The laying of the eggs took all of their limited intellect, leaving room for little else. They hadn't even ceased their activities when the strange craft appeared on the water.

David and Dian busied themselves taping the sequence of events, while the remainder of the group could not keep from laughing at the comical movements on shore. The saurians squatted, grunted, and let their yellowish, soft-shelled eggs fall with remarkable gentleness into the mud. How the clumsy creatures managed to avoid smashing their eggs with their feet or clubbed tails was beyond Bishop's understanding, but he didn't search for the answer too hard.

David and Dian continued to tape the events, and Dian's excitement was obvious in her expression, and even more so when she spoke. "This is marvelous. It's exactly what we were hoping to find. Gene, you have no idea how valuable these records will be."

Bishop chuckled. "No, Dian, I probably don't. And truth to tell, I'm not really that interested. But look, do you want to go ashore and start gathering?"

"Not yet," Dian replied, shaking her head slowly from side to side. "Later, maybe, but I'd rather mark this place and return later."

"That's probably the most sensible," David agreed. "The eggs will keep for a while, and the important thing at the moment is pinpointing locations of various suborders whose eggs should be taken back."

"Fine with me," Bishop said, shrugging. "It's your party. Just let me know when you've got enough."

"We will," David said with a chuckle, turning his gaze back to the squatting, grunting saurians on shore.

Chalfin gave the engines more fuel, and the boat spurted ahead, shortly riding on its hydrofoils once more. The ankylosaurs diminished in size as the group drew farther away.

Chalfin, at the request of his paleontologist passengers, increased the speed of the vehicle to slightly more than forty, the only real purpose of that being that the Grimsbys hoped to locate sites of the laying grounds of six different suborders as soon as possible, simply so they'd be sure of their positions.

It soon became evident that the increased speed was unnecessary, for on either side of the river, almost at regular intervals, were large dinosaurs of every shape and kind. And the farther the hydrofoil went, the more representatives of each suborder could be seen on the shores. Oddly, there were no small dinosaurs or even true reptiles.

Huge, skyscraping theropods squatted along the beaches, their multi-colored bodies contrasting with the brown and green of the mudflats. Surprisingly the huge creatures laid their eggs in an exceptionally gentle manner. Other flesh-eaters clawed at the wet ground with their powerful feet to dig their crude nests. Ceratopsia,

stegosaurs and ornithopods, all in their own ter-
ritories along the riverside, built nests and laid
eggs, according to the restrictions of their bodies.
The aquatic sauropods were the most curious of
all, prompting more than a few comments as
they ventured out of water and onto land.

"I think we've seen enough," Dian Grimsby
said at last, putting the videorecorder away as she
spoke. "We've got it all on tape, and a lot more
than we'd hoped for at that."

David Grimsby was happy, almost ecstatic. A
satisfied smile played across his face, and when
he looked from the spawning grounds of the
saurians to Bishop, there was gratitude in his
eyes. "You've done a great service for science,"
he said, "and for Dian and I personally, an even
greater one. We've located the laying grounds of
every suborder of dinosaur we wanted to find.
Now all that's left is to gather enough of each
group's eggs to accomplish the mission. I doubt
it'll take us more than a week to do that . . . perhaps less."

"And then," Dian said, smiling at her husband, "home to prepare for Dino-World."

"Dino-World," Bishop repeated softly, slowly.
"And a safer job than I've been working at for
the last decade. You know, I think I'm almost
looking forward to it."

David Grimsby nodded, then saw that his
wife's expression had changed, had become one
of mild perplexity. "What's wrong?" he asked.
"Post discovery letdown?"

"No." She paused before going on. "Not
that. It's just that, well I guess I expected an

abundance of wildlife, of every description imaginable. I assumed that since this is a virgin world, we'd see all sorts of strange creatures, and a lot of familiar ones too, for that matter. And the harmony of this world. Let's face it, when it comes to battles and violence, animals are almost as good as men. There hasn't been any of that here. I'm not disappointed, mind you, just . . . oh, maybe disillusioned." She chuckled softly. Then, "And I expected a lot more of everything that *is* here. The population really shouldn't be this small."

"Well," David started thoughtfully, "it's quite possible that what we're seeing here is the same type of thing that happened in our own late Cretaceous period."

"What difference does it make?" Bishop interrupted, shrugging. "We've located our eggs, we'll raise our own little beasties. You want millions of 'em, you'll *get* millions of 'em."

Dian chuckled, but went on, "The predator-prey relationship is out of whack with anything I've ever heard about or experienced. Considering the way the predators avoid attacking the vegetarians, it's remarkable they haven't starved to death long before this."

"Yes, something should be providing a regular diet," Dian went on. "It's ludicrous that a carnosaur must subsist on animals no larger than a dog. And beagle-size at that."

"These big ones seem to be over-specialized," Bishop offered. "That could be what's killing them."

"The mammals might be eating their eggs,"

Chalfin interjected. "Or maybe these big monsters are bright enough to know that they can't overpopulate, that birth control is the only thing that'll save 'em."

"They're incapable of thinking on that level," David said, almost as if he were explaining a very minor point to a questioning child, but strangely unoffending in his manner. "As a matter of fact, they hardly think at all, and their brains are little more than reactive tissue."

"Maybe they don't think very much at once," Chalfin went on, "but they live a long time, like turtles, and during that time they might think a great deal—accumulate data."

"Nonsense," David replied immediately. "Thinking's a gestalt, not cummulative. At least, not in the sense you're proposing."

"Just an idea," Chalfin defended himself, reluctant to give up entirely. "After all, we had problems with population excess; maybe the lizards did too."

There was a pause in the conversation, but it was short-lived.

"I still can't understand the carnosaurs subsisting upon mammals and a few of the smaller saurians and therapsids," Dian said. "They should be after those herbivores."

"It's amazing that the saurians catch the dog-like things," Chalfin said. "I've watched an *Allosaurus* work a field. The bloody thing didn't move too fast, but every time it reached down with those forelegs, it came up with something edible."

"They've had a lot of practice," Bishop reminded him. "But listen, enough of this. Let's head back. At the moment we're accomplishing nothing but a slow float out to sea." He chuckled. "We can start after the eggs tomorrow."

"Agreed," Dian said, and David nodded.

"There's one consideration," David started after a moment. "If the saurians are on the way out, life will be a lot easier for men, if any appear. I think these beasts would give prehominids a pretty rough time. Man could never have survived the age of reptiles; he's too slow, too weak, and far too edible."

While the hydrofoil sped upriver, Bishop turned his thoughts to David's last statement, wondering what men who developed on this planet would look like. Webbed feet and gills, perhaps, like those on Eridani IV? Or maybe like the Gandians, indistinguishable from Earth humans except for their canine teeth. He continued to ponder the possibilities.

Then, faintly, above the efficient hum of the engine and so shrill that it cut into his reverie, he heard a scream. And it wasn't a dinosaur! He scanned the shoreline and saw that they were passing a narrow place where the current moved at a considerable clip. Volcanic rocks formed the steep cliffs with cave mouths.

'Slow it down a bit, Jeff," he called out to Chalfin. "Keep her on the foils."

The scream came again, and over the edge of the cliff opposite them leaped a human figure. Human? Perhaps not, unless she had painted herself, for her skin was ruby red. She landed at the bottom of the two-meter cliff, and behind her came a toothy monster, one of the carnosaurs they had been discussing only a short time ago. The girl screamed again and stopped at the edge of the water. She turned and ran up the shore, and the carnosaur, scrambling and sliding, came down the bank in determined pursuit.

The girl's long strides carried her rapidly across the rocky riverbank, her ebony hair streaming behind her. She looked out toward the river, waved frantically, then started running again. And slipping and grunting, the carnosaur followed, his teeth more than obvious in those gaping jaws.

The girl would have no chance at all of staying ahead of the saurian. Then, suddenly, as she looked around to determine how close her pursuer was, she slipped, staggered, took one last step, and fell to the rocks. The spear she'd been carrying slipped from her hand and rolled away. She was looking into the eyes of the horror, her mouth open for another scream when, incredibly to those who watched from the river, she got to her feet and took one entirely unhesitant step toward the monster. It, too, had stopped and the orange fin along its back slowly became erect. It balanced on its walking legs, crest uplifted, head thrust out.

"Acrocanthosaurus," David Grimsby muttered, "but it's much larger. . . ."

"Can the lecture!" Bishop snarled. Then, turning toward the girl, he yelled, "Run! Run! We're coming!"

But the girl didn't run. Instead, like a sleepwalker, she moved toward the grinning jaws that were opening to receive her.

CHAPTER 6

Hearing Bishop's frantic bellowing to the woman, Chalfin had done the near-impossible. He had retracted the foils and beached the craft in a distance of less than twenty meters. Even before the sounds of the engine had died away, he'd picked up his rifle and was following Bishop and the two crew members from the boat and onto the rocks.

There were less than five meters separating the beautiful, red-skinned woman and the saurian when Bishop set foot on shore, and by the time he'd positioned himself to take even a half-decent shot, there were less than three meters between them, and the girl was still moving toward those grinning, gaping jaws of horror.

He wasn't totally prepared, but he had to get a shot off, and fast! He fired. The shot seemed to crease the creature's snout, but it was just a crease, barely enough to make the walking horror realize it had been hit.

Then the jaws were open and the girl reaching to climb into them—*climb into them*! his incredulous mind echoed—when a shot from over his shoulder struck the saurian's snout dead-center. The beast's great head arched backward, and its deep, gutteral growl became a roar of pain, rising until it was a loud shriek. The white teeth snapped closed less than half a meter from the girl's head; she was still reaching, but her arms were beginning to drop.

The predatory beast screamed again, turned to face the cause of its pain, and Bishop saw it frontally, almost as if the bellowing, pained creature was staring at him. His rifle lowered a bit, but he forced it back to his shoulder, drawing a careful aim. But again he thought the huge beast was staring at him—not the others, at him!—and he found his head was beginning to swim, almost as if something in his brain were being sucked from his skull.

He fired again, but his arms were shaking from the effort, and he missed. He was only vaguely aware of the sounds of additional rifle fire from behind him.

The saurian screamed in rage and fear once more, and its head lifted, breaking the line of vision it had held with Bishop. Bishop was once more in control of himself when he suddenly noticed that the huge beast had moved no more than a few meters away from the ruby-skinned girl; it was starting to move back to her. She would be crushed under those huge feet if she didn't move, and it didn't appear as if she was going to come back to her senses before she *was* crushed!

There were easily forty meters between Bishop and the girl when he threw his rifle down and started running toward her. "Cover me!" he screamed over his shoulder, forcing his legs to move faster to propel him across the volcanic rock.

For some reason he didn't have time to understand and wouldn't have understood with any amount of leisurely analysis, he didn't look at the saurian's eyes, but kept his own averted, concentrating on the red-skinned female, who only now looked like she was regaining at least an iota of self-awareness.

He heard the saurian scream as Chalfin and the others continued to fire, but he couldn't force himself to look up. Again the noises of gunfire and again the screams, rising, building, until it seemed all the world was nothing but enraged sound.

And still Bishop ran toward the girl—toward the saurian—hoping to reach her before the dinosaur trampled her or recovered from the gunfire enough to attack him.

The girl seemed to be gaining awareness, and suddenly, even as he ran over the uneven, rocky ground, Bishop could see that she was indeed fully alert. She appeared startled, as if she couldn't understand where she was, then instantly shifted to one of horror, and her mouth opened, her beautiful red features terrified and contorted in shock.

She screamed.

With a brief lull in the shooting the saurian heard the scream and looked to its left where it saw her. And Bishop, who had just reached her.

The saurian opened its jaws and snapped at them.

The rifle fire began immediately as Bishop leaped through the air and collared the girl, pulling her to the ground with him. They rolled over the rough rock, ripping his uniform and scraping the skin beneath the cloth.

He rolled only a few meters, then was on his feet, the girl in his arms. He dashed behind the saurian so it couldn't see him—it turned, ponderously, slowly, attempting to follow his erratic path, somehow he managed to avoid its thrashing tail.

From the time Bishop had begun his mad dash, Chalfin and the others had been firing at the saurian, but none of the strikes were direct, and none had been in the eyes or on the snout. Only the thick, scaly hide, received the glancing hits. Undoubtedly their aim had been affected by the sight of their skipper racing across the volcanic rock and fears that they would hit him.

With Bishop out of the way, they could concentrate better and began a steady stream of fire at the dinosaur. Bishop, when he reached them, dropped the woman and picked up his own rifle.

The saurian was screaming in agony now, its snout a bloody pulp and a few holes appearing around its neck. As the screaming, staggering beast started toward them, Bishop took careful aim and then, slowly, squeezed the trigger. Direct hit!

The creature's left eye exploded, and it roared in agony. It staggered, its massive tail crushing volcanic rock to powder, but it still continued toward them, weaving from side to side, refusing to fall, refusing to die.

Again Bishop took careful aim, fired, and smiled a tight, grim smile as the beast went down in a writhing, bellowing heap that twitched and shuddered with tremendous fury. Still Bishop and those under his command fired, round after round into the beast, until it's miniscule brain had been reduced to nothing. It gave one last bellow of pain and rage, twitched spastically for long seconds, then gave one final, bone-wrenching shudder and lay still.

Bishop, shaking almost as much as the saurian had, fell to his knees, sweat streaming out of every pore in his body. Then, remembering the girl, he got to his feet and turned to face her. She stood staring at him, her eyes still huge with amazement. He took her by a red wrist and led her over to the boat. Dian Grimsby gave the red body a glance, then made room for her to sit down.

"Gene," David started, and Bishop noticed the paleontologist's eyes were as big as the red-skinned woman's, "that was the—"

"Save it," Bishop panted, raising a hand and waving off the compliment, "save it."

"What are we going to do with her?" Chalfin asked, indicating with his hand the new addition to the group.

The girl's violet eyes were still wide, but she was beginning to accept the fact that she wasn't going to become an instant dinner for a dinosaur.

"Take her back to the ship," Bishop said. "We can't leave her out here." He looked at her more closely and decided he wouldn't want to leave her even if he could. Chalfin started the engine, and they were moving upriver again.

The girl's eyes now showed some sign of life other than fear or horror, and she was looking at Bishop with an expression so reminiscent of a Keane painting that he shivered. There was even the tear in the middle corner.

She was incredibly beautiful. Her face was smooth, with high cheekbones, a short straight nose, and a firm round chin. Her brows were curved and black, her forehead broad and smooth, and her ears small and set close to her head. Her jawbones were wide at the angles, giving her face a squarish rather than an oval shape, but her mouth was beautiful, and her teeth incredibly white. But her outstanding features were her eyes and hair. The hair was a glossy jet black mane of extraordinary thickness and luster. It hung to her waist where it was cut off square, leaving the impression that it would have grown to her feet had she permitted it. Her eyes were indescribable, so, naturally, he tried to describe them. Framed in extraordinarily long and thick lashes, her lids had a slight canthal fold that gave them a vaguely oriental look. The eyes themselves were a deep violet that varied with her moods. She was probably nocturnal, or lived where it was relatively dark. Her eyes and skin indicated that much. Yet she wasn't apparently bothered by the evening sun, and the light was bright enough.

Her body was perfection, naked except for a necklace of carnosaur teeth and a loincloth. It was an athlete's body; trim, taut, subtly curved, unbelievably smooth-skinned and virtually hairless. Her legs were long, her waist narrow, her shoulders wide and her breasts moderately sized and firm.

Her only defects were a few recent scratches and smears of mud, and the calluses on her lean feet and long-fingered hands.

Bishop sighed. Who said that a primitive had to be a slob? Pride of person need not be confined to fashion models. This girl was beautiful and knew it; and she took care to see that she stayed as beautiful as her gods and her genes had made her.

Bishop finished the inventory reluctantly, perfectly willing to go back for another reading, until he realized that she was conscious of his gaze and responding to it. Her eyes changed to a soft velvet with hints of gaiety and sweetness in their depths, and she preened herself subtly.

"She's after you, my boy," David said as he looked first at the girl and then at Bishop. "I haven't seen so blatant an exhibition since I taught paleontology at Rutgers to a class of sophomores."

"She's predatory," Dian said. "And she's beautiful. So watch out, Captain. She has an eye on you."

Bishop grinned. "I've been around," he said. "Spacemen get to a lot of worlds." Yeah, he thought, but never on any of them had he seen anything like this girl. She put the gold and honey Cassandra to shame. He could feel himself sweating. Her physical attraction was an aura. Yet Chalfin wasn't bothered, and the two crewmen were relatively indifferent and showed only the normal interest that any heterosexual male has for a scantily clad female of the same or similar species.

He wondered about the carnosaur teeth. If she had a mate or a boyfriend who could kill one of those beasts, he wouldn't want to meet the fellow. But however she had gotten them—and judging from her sacrificial virgin attitude toward the carnosaur she hadn't counted the coup herself—the necklace was the perfect barbaric foil for her beauty. It gave her an animal attractiveness that would otherwise be lost in her appealing innocence. Those eyes, he thought—a man could get lost in their depths and never emerge again.

With an effort, he turned his attention back to the river. The shoreline was whipping past as they swept up the stream toward the meadow in which the starship stood.

"It's astounding, no, surprising—well, unusual at the very least—" David's voice ran down a string of progressively less emphatic expletives, ". . . to find someone like her in a place like this."

"What's a nice girl like you doing in a place like this?" Dian mocked. "Don't tell me I'm losing my sex appeal." There was a thin wail in her voice.

"Dian, my dear, don't be a damn fool. I've resisted pretty girls ever since I taught in junior college. You're the one I wanted to marry, and you're the one I did marry."

"But she's so damnably exotic. I think I could dislike her very easily."

David laughed. "She has her eye on our captain. Didn't you notice how she displayed herself when he was looking at her?"

"How could I help it?"

"Don't you know that you're the only one as far as I'm concerned? Or isn't that enough?"

"It's more than enough," Dian said. She looked at the red woman with pity. "She's never had as much as I, and she may never have it. What matters if you're not loved?" Dian touched the bare red shoulders, and the woman, after looking at the older woman for a moment, put her hands on Dian's temples, smiled, and then suddenly hugged her and placed her head on Dian's breast. Dian looked down and her blue eyes suddenly were very bright. "Poor baby," she said softly.

"Benton Dakka never reported any humanoids," Bishop said. He couldn't keep his eyes off the girl, but Dian's expression made him feel uncomfortable. She looked positively maternal.

"He probably never saw them. They're almost sure to be nocturnal, and their early habitat was probably where there was a lot of infra-red radiation. Her color should be an excellent heat shield."

"They might be intelligent enough to keep out of Dakka's way." David said. "That man absorbed everything he touched. It's a wonder that there aren't any Dakkasaurs here."

"Ah . . . but there are! Those little ones that look like plucked chickens. He wrote that they were very tasty and he called them *Dakkasaurus satirus*." Dian smiled. "You must have missed that entry in his journals." She laughed and the red woman smiled and clung a little closer.

David chuckled. "Wouldn't you know it," he said.

"There are other good reasons they'd be afraid to show themselves," Bishop said. "I wonder how many have been included in the carnosaur dietary. That big fellow sure had an eye for her."

"I expect that she'd be right tasty." Chalfin grinned.

The Grimsbys nodded. The red woman shivered as though with a sudden chill. Dian looked at her curiously. "But . . . she couldn't possibly understand," she began.

And then the girl pushed Dian away with surprising strength. "Reeka!" She said urgently, pointing at the water ahead, "Reeka!" She pulled at Bishop's shoulder. A stream of liquid syllables poured from her as her pointing finger quivered. "Reeka!" she repeated, and this time the word was a scream of terror!

CHAPTER 7

As Leea's soul returned to her body, she looked about her with fear and wonder. She had never seen men like these with their bodies covered with such strangely colored skins. And this thing in which they rode, never had she seen its like before. She touched it timidly. It shivered as if the soul in it was cold. She had shaken like that on cold nights in unprotected shelters. But it shouldn't be cold, for it was swimming very fast.

She looked at the yellow-hair with the beautiful face, the one who pulled her from the reeka's jaws—beautiful except for his eyes and skin. His eyes were too small and the same color as the noon sky on a clear day. They made her uncomfortable. And his skin was pink instead of red. It was like the skins of those the Underwater People took; bleached and ugly. She wondered what it would feel like. But his hair was beautiful and his eyes were kind, and he was very strong. She remembered how easily he lifted her and put her in this swimming thing when the reeka had her soul.

And then, he and the others *had killed the reeka*! And they had done it rather easily. The wonder of it shook her. And these pale strangers felt neither remorse nor fear nor joy. It was as if they had forgotten.

But reeka do not forget, she thought with a wild surge of terror. Even though this enemy was dead, there were others.

Would she be safe in this tribe of strangers? She looked at the two gray-skins she sat between, at their wrinkled faces and graying hair. What was wrong with them? Were they sick and being carried to a Place of Dying by the others?

It didn't seem possible because there were no tears and no farewells. No, they belonged and were accepted. Strange . . . strange. Her mind refused the quantum jump. She had never before seen middle age, and old wasn't even in her language except in the sense of "long ago."

What would they do with her? Their weapons were terrible indeed. Would they take her as a member of their tribe? Maybe they needed women. There were none except the gray one on her left. If they needed women, she would choose the yellow-hair. He was big and strong and would protect her. Idly she wondered what it would be like to lie with one so strange . . . would she be brave enough to mate with one who charged a reeka?

Konu had killed one, but that had been an accident—and her people had turned the two of them out because of it, else there would be a plague of reeka in their land. But these folk were different.

The gray woman beside her was saying something to the gray man. She couldn't understand, but she caught the note of jealousy. She made the friendship gesture and embraced the gray woman to tell her that she was a sister, and that she had no desire for the gray woman's man. And then the woman took her in her arms and wept, and the feeling of love and tenderness that came from her filled Leea to bursting with its glory. Leea sighed and laid her head upon the woman's breast. She was at peace with them. She was accepted.

Leea well understood the look upon the yellow-hair's face. And despite its smoothness she knew that here was no beardless youth, untried in hunting, unskilled in love. Here was a man, and if these people wore no hair it was not because they could not. The blue cheeks and chin of one of the men behind her was testimony of that. She wondered how sharp the knife must be that took off his beard so smoothly—far sharper than her own, she guessed. She would never see her black glass knife again. She sighed. It had been a good blade, keen and beautiful with much magic; a blade to skin with, to carve meat from bones, to keep off males who would come in place of her mate. She must get another knife if yellow-hair decided to take her. And he would decide, of that she was sure.

It was nice to lie upon the gray woman's breast. It was warm and sheltered, like her mother's arms long ago when there was food and warmth and safety from the terrors outside the caves.

The hard-faced warrior with the gentle eyes— the one with the great ring in his two hands— was speaking to the yellow-hair. He looked at her and smiled. He had a nice smile, and suddenly everyone was talking in their strange language— such a noise! But it was all light and pleasant.

But into it came the feel of reeka. Ah . . . she was right! The reeka knew. It had marked them! She stiffened, screamed and tried to warn them, but they would not hear, they would not listen! What was wrong with them? Were they not conscious of the reeka, here, under them—NOW!

The plesiosaur surfaced underneath the skimming boat. The foils on the starboard side raked across the armored back and the craft tipped, lost flotation and crashed into the water.

Chalfin had moved instinctively with the first turbulence. He cut the switches, held the boat up for a second or two as the water slowed its speed, and instead of a crashing capsize, the upset was almost gentle.

Damn! he thought. Damn stupid clumsy lizard!

There was a swirl of water beside him. A snaky neck curled above him. A horrid, beaked face looked into his own. Yellow eyes gleamed. The beak opened and closed, and Chalfin felt a sudden blinding pain that turned instantly to darkness. He never knew that the saurian had decapitated him or that he was dead.

The others, thrown into the water by the capsize, swam back to the boat. Bishop, blaster in hand, searched the water for the cause of the catastrophe. Leea was clutching his gunbelt. The Grimsbys were already on the high side of the craft trying to tip it upright. The two crewmen were clutching the seat backs, their blasters out . . . but where was Chalfin?

The question was answered a moment later. The plesiosaur broke water and the trunk of the chief pilot was dragged to the surface. The beaked head struck down; the powerful neck raised the trunk aloft and shook it violently.

Something gave, and the grisly relic was hurled half a dozen meters away. The plesiosaur gulped and swam toward the floating body, its paddle feet sending whirlpools surging behind it.

"Chalfin! Oh my God!" Bishop screamed. His voice was agony. He aimed his hand weapon and fired. The blast caught the saurian at the junction of jaw and throat. A torrent of dark blood shot from the charred hole. The beak opened and Chalfin's body splashed into the river where it was immediately engulfed in a roiling mass of water and foam.

The saurian, its jaws dangling helplessly, fountaining blood that stained the water red, swam past them, already surrounded by gulping scavengers that consumed it even as it died.

The sight was enough to provoke superhuman effort. No one quite knew how they did it, but the boat was right side up and the two crewmen were working the bilge pump. The gray pair laid hold of Leea and pulled her over the gunwhale while Bishop, cursing and retching at the same time, cleared the steersman's seat and punched the starter.

The engine caught, and the pump quickly cleared the boat of water. Chalfin's quick reactions had saved the engine and the boat, and although the hydrofoils were ruined it still could float and move.

Leea, lying on the wet floorboards, looked at the quivering shoulders of the yellow-hair. The man—Chalfin?—was probably his friend, and he was mourning the dead as was proper. Yet—he had killed another reeka! And this one a sea reeka, which men seldom saw. If they were in the water they never lived to tell of seeing! Truly, this man was a warrior among warriors!

She came to her knees behind him and touched the back of his neck with gentle fingers. The shaking stopped. She touched his temples in the Gesture of Friendship, and as he turned to look at her, she touched his eyes in the Gesture of Love.

He smiled faintly and patted her head. A strange feeling overcame her. He didn't know what she had done. He thought she was trying to comfort him. But no woman comforts a warrior. She cares for his wounds, feeds him, loves him, bears his children, cares for his weapons, and sees that his life is pleasant, but she never comforts him. That is an act reserved for children. She sighed. Oh well, there are other ways a woman can let a man know she loves him. She would try those when the time was better.

The search party returned in silence, unloaded what was left of the boat's contents, and returned glumly to the *J-17*. Chalfin's death had cast a pall over their spirits.

"Tomorrow we'll repair the boat," Bishop said dully, "and as soon as it's repaired we will collect those damned eggs, and then we go home. Meanwhile, I'm going to get drunk." He stepped into the open air lock.

Leea, who had been eyeing the silver bulk of the spaceship with increasing uneasiness as they approached, gasped and shrank back. Her man was actually walking into the gaping jaws of this monster!

"Now what's wrong with you?" Bishop snapped.

"She's afraid, that's all," Dian said.

"I didn't ask you. I asked her." Bishop was being unreasonable. He knew it, but he had to snarl. He was at loose ends. He had seldom lost a man, and to have it be Jeff—that was too much!

Dian recognized the signs. She moved away and left Bishop to his pain. She could do nothing to ease it and maybe this red-skinned woman or Cassandra could.

"Well? Are you coming?" Bishop asked as he grasped Leea's wrist.

She pulled back, worried at the harshness of his voice.

"Dammit!" Bishop exploded. "I asked you. Now I'm telling you: *move!*" And then he jerked her forward, swung an arm under her thighs and carried her aboard. Leea knew this. A man carried his woman into their cave for the first time, and although this was a strange cave indeed, he had behaved properly. She stroked the strange blue skin of his arm and smiled.

The air lock guard grinned. "Where did you *pick* her up, skipper?" he asked.

"Shut up," Bishop snarled. "Button your mouth. Chalfin's dead. Lizard got him. Funeral services in two hours. Pass the word to the first officer." He stalked off into the ship with Leea following at his heels. They went through tunnels, up ladders, past strange places until finally they came to a wall that slid aside when her man touched it.

The sleeping cave within was unbelievable! Leea gasped, and she gasped even louder at the tall woman with red-gold hair and flawless cream complexion. But the gasp was more for what she wore than for the woman herself. Cassandra's clothes were masterpieces. She sewed them herself to pass time on the long trips through space, and the results were worth the effort. This was an informal lounging robe, subtly cut and embroidered and made of sheen fabric that changed color as the lights shifted over the prismatic threads. On some women it would merely be gaudy, but Cassandra triumphed over the gown.

The ivory and gold woman touched Bishop in a way that Leea fully understood.

"I've been waiting for you, Gene," she said, and then her eyes fell on Leea. "Hello now, who's this? My replacement?" She smiled. "I didn't think there were any humanoid natives here—and scarlet, too! My, she's a beauty, Gene. I always said you had good taste."

"Don't be bitchy, Cass," Bishop said. "I'm not in the mood for a fight. Chalfin's dead."

Her knuckles went to her mouth. "Oh, no!" she said. "What were you doing—rescuing the woman?"

"Something like that. Ask the Grimsbys. They were there."

"And what are you going to do with her?" Cassandra gestured at Leea.

Bishop shook his head. "I don't know. She's halfway adopted me, and I feel responsible for her."

"Like that old Chinese thing—save a fellow's

life and you're responsible for it from then on?"

He nodded.

"Well, she looks the part. There's something celestial about her and you can take that either way. Do you want me to move my things out?"

Bishop shook his head. "No," he said, "not now. Just get out."

"Exit Cassandra," she said. "Enter . . . hey— what's her name?"

"Damned if I know," Bishop said. "I never asked her."

CHAPTER 8

The crew was gathered in the control room. Everyone was there except Leea. Bishop stood tall and somber beside the pilot's chair. He wore his dress uniform.

"God gives, and God takes," he said. "And no man can say why. Jeffery Chalfin is gone from our company. In the best traditions of our service he died doing his duty. If it were not for him, we who have survived would not be here. We are assembled here to hold a service for the dead . . . yet somehow I cannot say it. For me, Jeff Chalfin is not dead. He lives in my memory and his spirit is the spirit of this ship. He has sat in this chair many times and has brought us home safely. He has put his imprint on these controls and on the starlanes he has traveled. To us who knew him, he will never die. So rather than mourn him as dead, let us think of him as a part of that greater life from which we have all come, and to which we must in our due time return."

He paused. "I ask you to pray with me," he said. "Even you who do not believe in God. For Chalfin did, and it would ease him—will ease him—to know that we appreciated him more than we could say when he was alive, and our feelings have not changed now that he is dead. Let us pray." And in a strange hushed voice Bishop said in the old speech, "The Lord is my shepherd, I shall not want. . . ."

At the end of the ancient prayer he stepped down and walked away, and it was a full minute before anyone moved. Probably no one but the

Grimsbys knew that the Psalm was truncated. It was not written in the new texts as Bishop had said it, and the captain edited it for his purposes. But the noble prose of a bygone age had an effect all the more potent for its antiquity.

"Bishop ... ah yes," David muttered. "A Bishop indeed. My God—how I've misjudged the man."

Dian wiped her eyes. "It was beautiful," she said softly. "When I die, my dear, have someone say those words over me."

The crew dispersed and went about their duties. The watches were posted and the ship prepared for bed.

BISHOP sat on his bed and looked at the woman's quiet face.

His stomach churned, but soon a different feeling swept over him. Could I *love* her? Her hands came up and touched his eyes, and for a moment he felt a sense of completeness, a feeling of belonging, a feeling of joy!

"Dear Lord," he said softly, "Is this what I have missed?" There was no answer. But somehow he knew that this time he had encountered someone he could never put aside.

Leea was happy. This nest was something she never dreamed existed, and her yellow-hair, her mate, her lover, was all she had imagined and more. He put Konu to shame in every way. How was it that this wonder had happened to her?

She smiled. Indeed, it had not been as difficult as she had imagined. He had need for her, and she had brought him peace. She would, of course, have to learn all about this strange place. But one thing at least was the same. A man loved a woman as she should be loved, and that was a start.

To educate a savage into the customs of civilized society was going to be a task, Bishop thought. But they had made a start. She learned what a bed was for, how the toilet and shower worked, and the mysteries of soap, perfume, and hairbrush. He knew that her name was Leea, and she knew that his name was Gene.

Well, at least the introductions were over; that was something.

Sue Madden knocked on his door and spoke to him of diseases and parasites and vectors—and Leea. Damn! Bishop thought, why did medics always have to try to frighten people? In their way, they were as bad as the Revisionists who wanted to go back to the days when liberty equated the right to meddle in everyone elses' business with license and freedom. But, of course, Sue was right. Leea would have to have a checkup and so would he.

He dialed for Cassandra.

"Good morning, sir," Cass's voice was formal.

"Cass, I need a favor."

"What?"

"I need some clothes for Leea."

"So that's her name. Don't you think you're going a bit too far? Aren't you satisfied with giving her my place?" Cassandra's voice was teasing.

"Please, Cass."

"Oh, all right. I have plenty of clothes and I can always make more. She ought to look marvelous in a white jump suit with black accessories to match her hair. Look . . . I'll be right over

with a few things and we'll make her beautiful—
that is if we can improve on perfection. That girl
makes me green with envy!"

"You're not mad?"

"Of course not. We were going to split anyway, and while I figured on a few more subjective
weeks, it won't make any real difference as long
as I can use your shower."

"The crew will think I'm running a harem."

"So what? Your reputation is ruined anyway—
no matter what you have or haven't done."

"Okay," Bishop said. "You get shower
privileges."

"Good. I'll be right over."

And so she was. She had several outfits and
her shower cap.

"Now get out of here, boss, while your girl and
I get acquainted."

"Leea," Bishop said. "Cassandra."

"Cassandra," Leea said.

"Leea," Cassandra said, and that was that. But
when he tried to leave, Leea refused to let him go.

"Clinging vine type, eh," Cassandra said.
"Didn't know you liked that kind."

"She's afraid," Bishop said.

"Of me? Don't be silly. I'm the competition,
not the enemy. She's no more afraid of me than
you are. Oh well, let's see what we can do with
her. You won't be in the way if you sit quietly."

Leea approved of the panties and admired the
brassiere, but it was the white jump suit that
brought the squeal of admiration. She, too, was
to have one of the strange skins, and it was so
beautiful! Whiter, even, than Cassandra's skin!

Cassandra started to reach for the necklace of saurian teeth. "She won't need these," she said.

"Leave them alone," Bishop replied. "I like them."

"Superior male; sexist, chauvinist pig," Cassandra muttered. "They make her look like a slave girl."

"That's none of your business. Just show her how to put those clothes on."

Cassandra did, and both the women got a great deal of amusement out of Leea's gyrations as she wiggled into Cassandra's skin tight creation.

"Can I have the shower now?" Cassandra asked.

"Help yourself," Bishop said. "We're going to visit your roommate."

"Oh?"

"Sue wants her to have a medical check. Said something about biological data and drug parameters."

"Ha, ha," Cassandra replied.

Leea didn't come off entirely clean. She was parasitized, which wasn't surprising, and she did harbor two viruses that could be pathogenic, but that was all.

"It's amazing," Sue said. "She's healthier than we are, and she has an almost perfect physique. Her reaction time is awfully fast, and outside of some slight differences in blood chemistry and the fact that she's a mirror image of us insofar as organ position is concerned, she's human to four decimal places. Her antigen and drug tolerance is the same as ours, too. But don't ever let her take a blood transfusion. It could kill her.

And, oh yes, her chromosome count is different; so you cannot have children—which should be a relief."

"Why?" Bishop asked, yet nevertheless he was relieved. Half-breed children had a hard time of it, even on compatible Earth.

"She'll be a little sick for awhile," Sue went on. "I've given her all the standard immunizations and have started her out on viracide. I hope she's potty trained because there's a healthy dose of polyfuge moving into her small intestine about now." Sue grinned unfeelingly. "Your girl is going to hate us both in about two hours."

Leea didn't hate anyone. She was far too sick and sorry for herself to feel any other emotion. At first she thought she was going to die. Finally she began to recover. It took three days, and in the meantime the boat had been repaired and the egg collection started.

In the meantime Bishop, Cassandra, and the Grimsbys had several conferences on ways and means.

"We won't have to guess about the next mission to this world," Grimsby said. "It'll be anthropological. The species Leea exemplifies would make a fascinating study. I've recorded her as *Homo sapiens rubrum*, but of course that will be changed. She's not really human, you know."

"I don't know," Bishop said. "What's human?"

Grimsby shrugged. "Ask a philosopher," he said. "I wouldn't know. I'm just a taxonomist and a paleontologist. I don't qualify; I just classify, and her skin and eyes alone would make her alien."

"I agree with the skipper," Cassandra said. "It's how one acts that counts, and she acts like a lady."

Bishop's eyebrows rose. He didn't expect Cassandra to defend Leea. For some reason, probably male vanity, he expected her to be bitchy and when she wasn't he was disappointed. He smiled wryly. In his own way, he was another Dian Grimsby—disappointed because the animals didn't fight.

"It hasn't taken her long to get used to the ship," David said. "That argues a fairly high intelligence and a considerable adaptability."

"More so than you might expect," Bishop said. "She understands, often without words. I think she may be some sort of a telepath."

"Empath, more likely," Grimsby replied. "She recognizes voice tones, facial and body cues and attitudes, and translates them into guides for her own conduct."

"She does seem to know things." Cassandra agreed.

"That could be why she acted so strangely when that carnosaur attacked her. Possibly she went into rapport with it," David said. "Or maybe it hypnotized her, like snakes are supposed to do with birds."

"They don't," Dian said. "That's superstition."

"At any rate she knows we don't intend to harm her," Bishop said.

"Not prematurely at any rate," Cassandra laughed. "But right now I wouldn't be too sure she looks on us as friends. Sue worked her over pretty thoroughly. I think she's unhappy because I'm always underfoot."

"She'll get over that," Bishop shrugged.

"I think we should teach her our language," Cassandra suggested. "It would make things much easier for all of us."

"I agree," David said. "If we could bridge the communication gap, she could tell us quite a lot on the trip home. I only wish that I had sense enough to have brought a neurosynthesizer. It's going to be a long job teaching her without mental imprinting to help us."

"Then you're in favor of bringing her back to Earth?" Bishop asked.

"Of course, if for no other reason than that she's a valuable specimen; she can tell us much more about Dakka VII than we could possibly learn in the short time we shall be here. And since we know she can vocalize, it shouldn't be too much trouble to teach her basic speech."

"I'll help," Cassandra volunteered.

"So will I," Bishop said. "But I haven't gotten very far."

"Like me Tarzan, you Jane?" Cassandra said.

Bishop grinned. "Maybe more like me Jane, you Tarzan," he said. "But she does learn names of things and people readily enough. She's smart."

Dian looked at David, and David looked at the ceiling; whatever Dian was going to say remained unsaid.

"You want to be tutors, too?" Bishop asked.

"Whenever you need our help," David said. "But not for the next few days. We'll be busy with eggs."

CHAPTER 9

"I'm not so sure you should go," Bishop said to David. "I wouldn't want what happened to Jeff to happen to you."

"Fortunes of war," David replied. "And besides, if we keep a better lookout, it might never happen again."

"We could use Leea to warn us," Dian said.

"No." Bishop's voice was flat. "She stays aboard ship." His tone said he would consider no suggestion that would bring Leea outside.

"Mind telling us why?" David asked.

"Personal reasons."

"So?"

"Not physical," Bishop said. "I'm fond of the girl, but that's not the reason. It's something you said."

"I?" David asked.

Bishop nodded. "You said she might have rapport with the saurians. If so, it obviously isn't a good rapport. With her aboard, Chalfin died, and I'm not going to lose any more people if I can help it."

"That's nonsense."

"Nevertheless that's my decision. And quite probably it would be Leea's if we could ask her. She doesn't like the saurians at all, and I don't blame her."

"Oh very well," David sighed. "I really can't argue with you; you are the captain."

"As far as the ship and the crew are concerned, I'm God Almighty. The Space Regulations give me discretionary power, and I will use it as I think best to promote the general safety of ship and crew."

"And passengers?"

"Only when you are aboard. Otherwise you can kill yourselves in any way you wish. But people I am responsible for will obey my orders."

"That G.A. in your initials, Gene, doesn't stand for either Gene Arthur or Guardian Angel or even God Almighty," David said. "It stands for Grouchy Authoritarian."

"Let's get moving on the egg collection," David suggested. The foundation wants at least thirty-six eggs—six from each suborder. Personally, I think there should be more. We have plenty of room and no weight problem on the ship. I'd like to take a larger sample."

"That's your decision," Bishop said. "But you don't want to overcrowd the park. Now do you have any preference as to whom you'd like to take with you on this expedition?"

"You, of course, the same two men who went before, if they wish to come, and Dian and myself. You can pick the other man."

"I'm going to ask for volunteers," Bishop said, "and I'm going to stay here. Someone has to stay behind who knows the route you'll travel. I'll assign Lieutenant Edwards to the boat as commander. He's smart and experienced and will get you where you want to go."

"May I go too?" Cassandra asked.

Bishop nodded.

Adams, to Bishop's gratification, volunteered to go. Wilson opted to stay and was replaced by Guthrie from engineering.

The Grimsbys weren't exactly happy with the arrangement, but Bishop wanted to have everything ready for a quick departure and would allow no one else to take the responsibility of preparing the ship for flight.

So while the engineering staff cleaned out the jets and checked the drives and converters, Bishop and the Glory Hole staff conducted a meticulous second-echelon inspection of the control room circuitry.

THE days passed smoothly. The ship was inspected. Minor repairs were made; jets were cleaned and refocused. Instruments were recalibrated, and all the myriad things a ship needed to have done to be space-ready were done.

Leea was an interested spectator. She went from group to group and watched the men and women work. What they were doing was obviously important, but she had no idea what it was.

The boat crew was efficient and adequate, and after the first day the Grimsbys had nothing but praise for their helpers. Bishop rotated the officers and crew, always keeping at least one old crewman aboard. It served two purposes: it gave the men an excursion, and it returned the specialists to their jobs on the ship without disturbing the inspection and repair routine too greatly.

As the eggs came aboard Leea became increasingly uneasy. She stayed closer to Bishop and began looking around as though something were hiding in the corridors of the ship. "Reeka," she said once. "They here. I feel." And then she lapsed into a worried silence that expressed itself in close physical contact, as though she needed his physical support. While this wasn't at all distasteful to Bishop, it did his image no good and he was forced to banish Leea to his quarters while he supervised the work.

To Bishop's surprise there were no more attacks or incidents at the egg depositories. The saurians paid the Grimsbys and their boat crew no attention, and the egg gathering went on until the last container in the specially refrigerated cubicle was filled.

When the last egg was collected, the last plant dug and the last samples of the smaller animal life netted and put into coldsleep, Bishop took a rifle and three men on a hunting trip. They came back with a small bipedal saurian weighing about thirty kilos and looking like a plucked turkey.

AND that night the crew feasted on one of the most delicious meats they had ever eaten.

"That beast ought to be domesticated," Cassandra said with a smile. "Anything that good should be preserved."

The Grimsbys and the crew said nothing. They only ate.

"A wine sauce would make it a bit better," Bishop suggested.

"Nothing could make it better. It would merely be different," Cassandra said.

"We're eating *Dakkasaurus satirus*," Dian Grimsby said.

Leea said nothing. She busily ate until her

stomach bulged and her eyes became dull with food.

Bishop watched her, a trifle surprised at her capacity for saurian. Well . . . she ate them; they ate her. It was a sort of mutual activity.

It wasn't really a farewell dinner after all. It was a farewell gorge. And take-off, which Bishop had scheduled for 19:00 hours, was postponed until morning. Too many of the ship's company were incapacitated by overeating.

Bishop patted Leea's shoulder and she looked up at him, licked the bit of roast from her lips and sighed contentedly.

"Reeka?" Bishop asked, pointing at the remains of the main course.

She shook her head. "Alora kagga," she explained and patted her round stomach. "Good." She waited a second then held her nose. "Reeka bad." And having made her point clear she stood up and walked slowly off to Bishop's cabin.

When he found her a half hour later, she was curled up on the bed, snoring happily.

CHAPTER 10

The lift-off wasn't routine. Bishop missed Chalfin every minute of the five required to put the *J-17* in orbit. It wasn't that he didn't have confidence in Blakely, the copilot, but he and Jeff Chalfin had worked so closely together that they were virtually one person, and with Blakely, none of the subliminal cues and responses were there.

As a result the take-off was a little ragged, not really dangerous, but different enough from the previous smooth lift-offs to make both Bishop and the crew uneasy.

It was time he retired, Bishop thought as Blakely put the ship into a parking orbit around the planet in preparation for the work necessary to prepare the ship for space.

Theoretically, nothing needed to be done, since the crew was accustomed to zero gravity and could operate in it with only slight loss of efficiency. But the drawbacks of a free-fall existence for several subjective weeks made gravity imperative. Since weight was achieved by spinning the ship on its long axis, the furniture and controls had to be reoriented; what were decks and ceilings when the ship was on the ground became walls in space, and the walls became decks.

It was peculiar and a little disquieting for those who were new to space to look upward at the central axis of the ship and pass from zero gravity along the axis to a light but comfortable 0.2G at the periphery. But the worst thing was tnat all the furniture and controls in the inhabited part of the ship had to be rotated through an arc of ninety degrees, since the outer walls became the deck once spin was applied to the ship.

On the passenger vessels, there was a different means of obtaining artificial gravity, but the equipment was heavy and expensive and took up valuable space. A freighter simply went into orbit and stayed in free-fall while the crew shifted the furniture and controls from the landing position to the flight position.

It wasn't too hard to do underzero gravity as long as one understood that the weightless equipment had mass and that bulky pieces had to be moved slowly. The crew must undo the latches that held the furniture and instrument modules to the walls and floor, unplug the wiring, rotate the whole unit through an angle of ninety degrees, and relatch and replug it into the receptacles in what were once the walls. It was a sort of musical chairs, and the two major groups aboard ship—navigation and engineering—had friendly competition—and bets—on who could rerig faster. But in a surprisingly short time the whole human-inhabited interior of the ship could be completely reoriented.

It made no difference as far as the cargo of seeds, fruits, plants, and animals were concerned. The fauna could be left in coldsleep and it didn't really matter whether the carefully packed plant material was lying flat or on end. The eggs, however, were a different proposition. The Grimsbys had packed them carefully in a refrigerator module that could be rotated to keep them upright.

Leea stood the increased weight of lift-off quite well, her athlete's body easily accommodating to the 2G acceleration, but when the ship went into orbit—and she slowly floated out of the bed, propelled by the resilience of the mattress—she panicked!

Bishop, who was expecting something like this, took off from the stanchion he was holding, swept through the control room hatch, banked off the corridor wall and killed his momentum with a neat somersault, cushioning the effect with his soft-soled space boots and bent knees.

Holding onto the grabrail, he jerked his door open, took one look at Leea kicking and squirming weightlessly, jerked a sick bag out of his utility belt, and jammed the open end over her gasping mouth.

"Okay, let it go," he said.

Leea was suddenly and gaspingly sick. She had never experienced true weightlessness and disorientation before, and the combined effects were like those that followed the eating of too much *kifa* fruit.

Bishop sealed the bag and handed her another. She shook her head. He held the bag out to her again. Obediently she took it and put it to her mouth. He laughed, took it from her and tucked it into the waistbelt of her jump suit.

She smiled weakly. This was a very strange place. She wondered if she would ever get used to it. Now she was floating in air.

He put his arm around her and held her gently. She clung to him, but when nothing else dreadful happened she slowly relaxed. After a minute or two she didn't feel quite so queer and her stomach felt a little better.

"Got you just in time," Bishop said. "Another second and we'd never have gotten the place cleaned up. You can't imagine how that stuff spreads in no weight." He grinned. She probably didn't understand a word he said—which was no loss. He pointed at the bag. "Sick bag," he said. He pointed at his mouth and made etching motions.

She nodded.

He stopped. A strange expression crossed his face. Suddenly he pulled another bag from his belt. From somewhere down the corridors of time he could hear the space medic's dry voice. He remembered his first experience with weightlessness as a cadet.

"Space nausea, gentlemen, an be overcome. But you should always remember that space is not a normal human environment. Even with experience, your body will always be on the borderline of nausea until your physiology has stabilized. So do not do things that might aggravate. . . ."

"Ulp!" Bishop said.

Leea watched him, and then she laughed. He looked so funny and so unhappy with himself.

"I hope the crew never hears of this," he muttered as he sealed the bag and dropped the pair of them into the pneumatic tube leading to the drive. Since anything served as reaction mass, the material wouldn't be wasted. "As for you, my girl, don't ever expect me to demonstrate space sickness again."

Leea smiled doubtfully. There was an odd note in Gene's voice, neither kind nor angry, and she wasn't quite sure what it meant.

She clung to his arm as he drew them out of the door. "There will be a couple of men along to reorient the cabin," he said, "and you'd be in the way, so you might as well watch the fun."

He kicked off and they floated down the corridor. Leea relaxed. This was fun! They banked off the far end and floated through the control room door and into the confusion. The Glory Holers were trying to beat the Black Gang. Engineering almost always won, but Control never ceased trying. Computers swam across the room. Vision tanks rotated ponderously. Control chairs twisted in midair as the struggling men and women moved them into place, dogged them down, and plugged their wiring into the alternate sockets.

Leea clung to a stanchion and watched the confusion as Bishop kicked off into the scramble and helped move segments of the main control board into place.

They were just locking the last control chair to the astrogation board when a voice came over the annunciator.

"Set," it said.

"Damn," Bishop replied. "We could have gotten them this time if I'd been here."

"What happened?" Cassandra asked. "Did she upchuck?"

Bishop nodded.

"You get there in time?"

He nodded again.

'That's a relief. For a moment I was afraid there'd be no more showers." Cassandra eyed Leea critically. "She looks okay now."

"I think so. Anyway she now knows what a bag is for." He kicked off toward the far side of the room and strapped into the control chair in front of the main board. "Stations everyone," he said into the annunciator. "Prepare for instrument check."

In seconds, the disorderly melange of bodies became a smoothly efficient unit as the components of the Glory Hole reported.

"Astrogation, all green, sir," Cassandra said.

"Drives green, sir."

"Converter green, sir."

"Security—two red, sir."

"Where?"

"Cth leak in drive, sir. One component in science cabin not secure."

"See to it, Harris."

"Yes, sir."

Bishop flipped a switch on his console. "Engineering, this is the captain."

"Aye, sir."

"Your report was a little premature, Allen."

"Sir?"

"You have a leak in your drive lattice. You're bright red up here."

"We're green down here, sir."

"Check it out."

"Aye, sir."

"Hey! Maybe we beat them after all," Harris said.

"Continue report," Bishop replied.

"Quarters green, sir."

"Services green, sir."

Allen's voice came over the annunciator. "We have a malfunction, sir," he said.

The Glory Hole cheered.

"Well, see to it," Bishop said. "Report when clear."

"Aye, sir."

Leea watched, wide-eyed.

"Science room green, sir," Harris said. "Those people are merely slow."

"Engineering to Captain," the annunciator squawked.

"Bishop here. Go ahead."

"We'll be about an hour, sir. We have a defocused jet."

"Why?"

"Because some butter-fingered lamebrain dropped a wrench, sir."

"Speak to him about it—or is it her?"

"Him, sir. And don't worry, sir; he won't do it again."

"Stand by," Bishop said. "Secure stations."

He unstrapped and sailed across the room to Leea. "Well, we're ready to go when Engineering gets the repairs done. Meanwhile, let's go to the common room and teach you something about zero gravity." He took her arm and moved into the corridor. "Cass," he said, leaning back through the door, "how about coming down to common and helping me with this groundhog?"

"It'll be a pleasure," Cassandra said.

"I'll bet you one thing," Cassandra said as they sailed down what once was the main manlift.

"She'll learn fast once she gets the hang of it. I'll give you two to one that she'll be handling herself all right before the Black Gang gets that jet refocused."

"You're on," Bishop said. "Five dollars."

He lost, for by the time Engineering reported that the malfunction was repaired, Leea was sailing back and forth across the common room as though she had done it all her life. It was an exhilarating experience and she couldn't get enough of it. She quickly evaluated the forces involved in weightless maneuvering, and her superbly responsive body did the rest.

"Lord! I thought she'd be good, but not that good," Cassandra said with envy as she watched Leea carom off the far wall, do a neat back flip and hit the near wall feet first, come off the ceiling and hit the deck with scarcely a jar. The red girl was laughing, her violet eyes bright with excitement.

"We'd better go back," Bishop said reluctantly. He had delighted in watching her and was half sorry he could not spare more time, but the *J-17* had a date with a transition point somewhere out in space between the fourth and fifth planets of the double sun. At the slow interplanetary speeds that they would be traveling, it would be several days before they made conjunction.

CHAPTER 11

Leea was put on a crash course in language during the voyage to Earth. Her capacity to grasp words and their meanings proved remarkable. Bishop attributed her rapid mastery of basic language to a keen intelligence, an active interest in the wonders around her, and a talent for extracting meaning from gestures and subliminal signals. She was a quick student, and what she learned she retained. Since she was obviously more capable of learning Bishop's language than he was of learning hers, the latter idea was abandoned altogether and all efforts were concentrated on teaching her English.

Before too many standard days had passed, the refugee from Dakka VII was already using her limited English vocabulary. Cassandra Wecklos proved to be most influential to Leea's education, and surprisingly the two women developed a genuine friendship for each other, a feminine equivalent of the relationship that had existed between Bishop and Chalfin. While Bishop was able to teach Leea the meaning of basic words necessary to conversation, Cassandra taught her abstract terms and the nonverbal signs and cues that are as much a part of communication as words. Between them they brought their willing and intelligent pupil across the quantum jump from translation to speech, and while her vocabulary was slender, it increased day by day. Her comprehension, in fact, was so much greater than her communicating abilities that she was continuously frustrated. If she could read, Cassandra thought,

Leea would soon be as fluent as any of them. If there was anyone who could use a few neurosynthetic treatments and the so-called "instant education," Leea was the girl. It was too bad, Cassandra thought for the twelfth time, that they didn't have a machine and an operator aboard.

Leea would not use the term Dakka VII for her world; Erigon was the land, the world in her language, and Erigon it remained. Presently everyone in the crew called the dinosaur world Erigon.

WHILE Cassandra educated the woman from Erigon Bishop used the time to visit with the Grimsbys. He was not entirely happy with the outcome of their expedition. Chalfin's death bothered him, and Leea's reaction to the eggs bothered him more. He made a pest of himself by interfering with their work of codifying and evaluating the data they had gathered on Erigon, but he persisted, and oddly enough the Grimsbys didn't resent him.

On one of these occasions, the paleontologists were examining the refrigeration containers in which the dinosaur eggs were stored. David was checking the eggs with a candling device to make sure that the temperature was low enough to prevent growth, while Dian was using an organic detector calibrated to Erigonian tissues to make sure the potentiality for life existed in the eggs. Bishop wondered what would happen if by some mischance the eggs proved to be dead. They would probably demand that he return, fuel, hyperspace and navigation problems notwithstanding. They were as devoted to those eggs as a pair of mother hens.

Bishop eyed the busy husband-and-wife team and said, "Strange, isn't it—the way a woman like Leea, who's faced so many horrors, should fear these harmless eggs."

"Oh?" answered David, raising an eyebrow and wrinkling his forehead. "You're on that tack again." He stepped away from the containers and turned toward Bishop. "I see you still haven't been able to convince her that she has nothing to fear from this section of the ship."

"Correct," said Bishop. "And it bothers me, although the more I think about it, the more the things you told me don't entirely make sense."

Dian put the last egg containers away and joined her husband. "What did David tell you?" she asked.

"Compulsions," said Bishop. "You were talking about them, too, Dian. You were trying to explain about the immobility that held Leea when that carnosaur came out of the woods. You said that life on Erigon probably evolved with its own unique set of checks and balances so the big carnivores wouldn't go hungry, even though they didn't attack the other dinosaurs. But I wonder. . . ."

Dian's eyes were amused. "Wonder? About what?"

Bishop had no intention of stopping. The problem interested him; more so because Leea was involved, but until now he hadn't the time to give it proper attention. Tricky astrogation was required to find a transition point for entering hyperspace that was properly aligned to bring them out somewhere within the vicinity of Earth. Transition was now over and the ship was loafing along on automatics at some two hundred lumes in the middle red of Cth. Now that only standard watches were necessary, the crew—and the captain—had time to spare. The biggest problem now was boredom, and Leea's terror of the stored eggs was a sufficient stimulus for Bishop to continue asking questions. "It occurred to me," Bishop said, "that there might be more to this reeka business than merely Nature's method of providing a proper diet for carnosaurs. It could be something else—something that we haven't considered."

"Such as?" asked David, the skepticism in his voice matching the expression on his face.

"Such as. . . ." Bishop paused, carefully considering his next few words. In consequence, he weasled, and it didn't come out at all the way he wanted. "Well, let me put it like this: remember when we first touched down on Erigon and that first group of lizards congregated around the ship?"

"Of course," Dian said, "That's a sight this fossil-hunter will never forget!"

"There were five of them, remember? Two carnivores and three herbivores. According to the paleontology books and what you've told me, Earth's carnivorous saurians didn't associate with their own kind. They had territorial imperatives, like bears and cougars. But the two flesh-eaters that came calling on my ship not only associated with each other, but with three potential dinners as well, and one of those dinners was a relatively defenseless marshland grazer."

David nodded. "True," he said. "But I thought we should attribute their odd behavior to physical factors such as different gravity, different components in the atmosphere, the two suns—that sort of thing. Let's face it, Erigon's saurians are somewhat different from the dinosaurs of Earth, and I wouldn't dare presume that their habits aren't also different. Besides," his eyes twinkled, "it seemed to me that eating the mammals, therapsids, and reptiles would be a much easier way to make a living than attacking the living tanks of their own kind. And you saw that they didn't have any hesitation about eating a dead saurian no matter whether it was herbivore or not. Personally I think it was the two suns and their shadow patterns that caused the saurians not to attack each other."

"Two suns! Ha!" Bishop snorted. "That's a thoroughly convenient garbage can for things we can't or won't explain. I think we've been using those two suns as a substitute for analysis and reasoning. Whenever something doesn't fit into our preconceived patterns, we drag out those two damned suns and let it go at that. But even *if* those suns and Erigon's other peculiarities have produced some aversion in these creatures to attack or eat others of their kind, why didn't those lizards go after us? They sure went after other mammals, including Leea."

"Maybe we smell different," Dian said.

David scratched his head. "Dian could be right except that the plesiosaur ate Chalfin. Of course, that was in the water and there might be a different set of parameters involved. But I *have* wondered about that. The saurians obviously eat mammals. We saw them snapping them up in the meadow, and that carnosaur on the beach was ready to eat Leea. Of course, it wasn't very active about it."

"It didn't have to be," Bishop said. "She just stood there."

"I won't be the one to suggest that it just wasn't hungry," Dian said with a wry smile. "Nor will I offer the same suggestion for the carnosaurs in our reception committee. They were working the little creatures over fast enough once the committee dissolved."

"I think those flesh-eaters must be constantly hungry," Bishop said, "and a nice haunch of brontosaur would always be acceptable. A group of humans shouldn't be bad either, but those two land-sharks didn't bother us at all."

"The twin suns *could* have refined their tastes even more," David said. "Maybe the lizards have an aversion to mammals that are not indigenous to Erigon. Those suns could—"

"Oh nuts," Bishop fumed. "I suppose the suns also made them respond to cues! As soon as I said something about their being so friendly, they suddenly began to snap at each other—and it was lousy snapping!"

David's eyes wandered until their gaze came to rest upon a section of shiny, gray floor near Bishop's boots. His voice was pensive. "You know, at the time the same thought struck me. But somehow it got shoved into the back of my mind with a lot of other thoughts. Now that I think back on it, it does seem that those animals began to fight on cue." He shook his head. "But that can't be. They simply don't have enough brains to do that. No, it's probably something else. Maybe it's seasonal. We weren't there long enough to examine that hypothesis."

"It was as though they staged their battle for our benefit," Bishop said.

"I know you feel that way," Dian said. She turned to her husband and then back to Bishop. "But I didn't get that idea at all. It was about midday and it was almost too hot to breathe. I don't think they had the energy."

"They ate the small creatures," Bishop said.

"But that was different. It wasn't hard to gobble them up. They almost begged to be eaten. But Ceratopsia is a different story. Look, I might eat a candy bar but I wouldn't eat an armadillo. It's the same analogy."

"Maybe . . . and maybe not," said Bishop, "but there's more about that so-called battle. Chalfin was right when he said he'd seen better and more realistic fights at the wrestling matches on Earth, where human wrestlers put on a show to please the customers."

"I don't think we're competent to judge," David said. "Dian and I were hopelessly excited about seeing the Mesozoic come to life. You and Chalfin were looking for trouble, and the others only wanted to get back to the ship and away from something they were at least half afraid of. You'll have to forgive us but I'm afraid Dian and I have both been guilty of falling into the classic absent-minded professor syndrome. But you should understand the sort of lives we lead, how such an event as landing on a Mesozoic planet could cloud our thinking. But now, this far removed from Erigon, maybe I can consider the situation with more objectivity and without the excitement I felt back there. And I'll try. But it probably won't get us very far. It may have to wait until the eggs hatch and we have some live specimens to work with."

"You should also remember what happened during our second hydrofoil excursion," added Dian. "Not one of those animals made any attempt to stop us when we gathered up their eggs. They simply let us pass as if they never even saw us. But before that, after we brought Leea into the boat, a plesiosaur attacked and created havoc. Why did that one saurian attack us while all the others left us alone? Maybe the sea serpent wanted Leea and not us."

"It won't wash," Bishop said. His voice was stubborn.

David interrupted. "Try this for size," he began. "If the saurian was prompted to attack by the presence of Leea, it is probable that some kind of psychic bond exists between the creatures of Erigon. Leea's presence could have attracted the *Plesiosaurus*; as I think of it, Leea was the only strange element in the boat." He smiled depreciatingly. "I'm not really Sherlock Holmes as you can see."

"It's better than the twin-suns theory." Bishop's voice was sarcastic.

The Grimsbys were silent.

Bishop sighed. "This isn't going to get anywhere, but before we decide that Leea's presence on the hydrofoil answers all questions, remember who died. It *wasn't* Leea."

"Hmmm. . . ." nodded David.

"The beast did get Chalfin, but he was next to Leea," Dian said. "And then it practically let us kill it with hand weapons. It wasn't half the trouble the carnosaur was."

"Whatever happened on Erigon is your baby," Bishop said soberly. "None of the rest of us have the knowledge. But Leea is terrified of eggs she's never seen, and the behavior of those beasts was unnatural by our standards. I don't buy the twin-sun hypothesis. There must be some more rational explanation. You two ought to work on it."

"We will," David promised.

Bishop tapped the wall of the cubicle that held the eggs. Leea knows they're here, and I'll bet *they* know she's here!"

"Then Leea could give us the answer to all this," said David.

"Maybe," Bishop said. "I wish she knew enough of our language to tell us what we should know! What we need is a neurosynthesizer." He shrugged and walked away.

"Persistent devil, isn't he?" David said to Dian as he watched Bishop's retreating back.

"He's worried."

"There's nothing to worry about," David said.

Dian sighed. "You don't believe that twin-sun nonsense you were telling Bishop, do you?"

"Of course not. No more than I believe that Leea can sense life in these eggs, or that dinosaurs put on a show for our benefit. You must remember, dear, that spacemen are all superstitious, that Bishop is hurt over Chalfin's death, and that hyperspace is a strange place. And that's the way it is with Bishop. He isn't seeing reality."

"Thank you David. You ease my mind," Dian said. "I can't help worrying."

"Don't," David told her.

CHAPTER 12

Whatever concept Leea had of time on Erigon was lost in the timelessness within the *J-17*. But she was aware that many subjective hours and days had passed since she left her home world. This did not trouble her, for like most primitives she was aware of time but not bothered by it. And there was the compensation of being with the yellow-hair who was called Gene Bishop. In her simplistic outlook, that was all that mattered.

Leea wanted to please Gene. She learned to walk with the odd hip-thrusting gait of the Earth-women and tried to forget her free, long, woods-man's stride. She frequently brushed her glossy black hair to bring out the sheen she knew Bishop admired. She wheedled Cassandra into making her borrowed uniform fit as perfectly as Cassandra's masterpieces.

She walked across the control room deck, her arm linked with Gene's, her smile as sweet as his was broad. She had already grown accustomed to many of the wonders of the craft, for Gene and Cassandra spent their free time teaching her and she was a quick student. She was pleased with her progress in learning the Earth people's language. She understood them well enough to relax in their presence.

"Gene," she asked on one of their promenades, "where is Earth?" Her dark eyes were intent as she waited for his answer. She desperately wanted to absorb all the knowledge she could about these strangely dressed people and the even stranger enclosure in which they lived. Still, she found it difficult to comprehend that this place called the *J-17* was actually traveling to the stars and not resting upon her own world.

"Leea," said Gene, "I'll try to show you, but don't blame me if you don't understand. I'm not a teacher, and spaceflight between the stars isn't something that everyone can learn. Actually, I'd be a fool to try."

Leea's smile broadened and took on a tiny Mona Lisa quirk at its corners. "Okay, so I'm a fool," Bishop said. He led her to the chart room and the tank that occupied a sizable area of gray wall. He checked the astrogation figures and punched the data code into the computer. The tank darkened, and dots and circles appeared in its velvet depths, each with a set of tiny hieroglyphics. As Leea watched, the entire picture moved toward them and off the tank's surface to be replaced with other dots and circles and hieroglyphics that formed in the depths of the tank. "Those are stars and planetary systems we are passing," he said. "Off to the left there is a globular cluster. That's something to avoid; that's why it's red."

"Am I something to avoid?" she asked. "I am red."

He grinned. "You're not a globular cluster," he said.

"Where is Earth?" she repeated.

"It hasn't come into the tank yet, and it won't for maybe another week."

"But. . . ."

"Okay, okay. I'll try to show you." He opened the drawer in the navigation desk and produced some paper and a pencil. He set the paper on the desk and drew two tiny, separate circles upon it. He placed a dot between them.

"Now look," said Gene, beckoning with the pencil.

Leea moved closer to him, interpreting his words and gestures. She exhibited a surprising understanding. When he smiled, Leea felt pride, and she also hoped he could smell the scent of the perfume Cassandra had given to her. "Earth?" she asked.

Gene pointed to the first of the spheres. "This is your world, Erigon," he explained. "This is where you lived; do you understand?"

Leea considered the words. She read his feelings, his attitude, and made the quantum jump from a circle to a planet. With a smile, she lowered her head, then raised it quickly and pushed her hair back over her shoulders. "It's a little thing on this paper," she said.

Again he indicated the marks on the paper, this time pointing at the dot. "This is the *J-17*," he added. "We are no longer on your world. We're right here." He gestured at the walls, pointed to the dot. "Inside this ship, the *J-17*."

The jump from dot to ship was easier this time, for she remembered the huge, bright object with the open mouth into which she was carried after her ordeals with the flesh-eaters. "The *J-17*," she repeated, pronouncing it slowly and distinctly. "It has eaten us and we are in its belly."

"In a sense," agreed Gene, giving her smooth arms a gentle squeeze of reassurance, "but it won't harm us. Instead, it protects us. We would die if we were not inside this ship. And the *J-17* is running past the stars to my world, the one we call Earth."

This was beyond her comprehension. "How can you run past the stars?" she asked. "Reeka and *Fleeya* fly, but they don't go that high." Saurians and insects, he translated as he wondered how he could possibly tell her about Reimann space, hyperspace converters and inertialess drive. He decided to oversimplify. She would have years on Earth to learn the finer details if she wished.

"So reeka applies to pterodactyls, eh? No, Leea, there are many other things that fly. We call them birds, aircraft, and spaceships. And right now we're flying in a spaceship that goes so fast and so strangely that even I, who run it, do not know how it travels. We fly much higher, much farther and much faster than any reeka could hope to travel. And the ship does not tire or need to rest. We are flying away from the place where you lived to the place where I live."

"Earth?"

"Earth," he said. "It will be your new home. It is a strange place, but there are no reeka. He moved his finger to the right, away from the dot representing the *J-17*, and rested it upon the second circle. "Here." Bishop jabbed his finger hard against the second circle, emphasizing it. "This is Earth. This is where we go."

"Earth?" asked Leea. She was getting repetitious, he thought, but he liked to talk to her. She was more attentive than most women and, despite her persistence, was not unpleasant.

Gene nodded. "It is a huge ball of land and water hung in the sky. Do you understand?"

Leea felt her heart beat faster. For she understood far more than he thought. Now was her chance to reveal to this man she loved that she was learning. She retraced his finger movements with her own. "Home . . . ship . . . fly . . . Earth." she repeated, "My home, the ship, it flies to Earth!"

Gene held her in arms that were even stronger than those of her former mate. They could have killed Konu, but they held her tenderly and she felt his possessive love for her. Almost savagely he kissed her, and for a moment she returned the pressure of his lips and thoughts of love. But then Leea pulled herself away. "Tell me more," she insisted, feeling her brow tense and her eyes dilate as her mind opened.

"I guess I'll have to. We'll be landing on Earth in a few more days."

She sweated with the effort to understand. It was hard to catch words and feelings when he spoke so quickly.

"After all," Gene continued, "you will enter a world different from anything you know. A preview will be good."

"What is preview?"

"This. Bishop opened one of the storage compartments and removed some boxlike objects and a miniature screen, which glowed with a bright light. "These are holograms of Earth scenes, Leea. They are pictures, previews of what you will see."

He slipped something into the device and the

screen became the colorful three-dimensional scene that Leea associated with "real" seeing. She gasped at this newest marvel. It showed a series of steep mountains, of fantastic cliffs and heights, gleaming silver in the sunlight with a majesty not present in her flatland world of shallow seas, jungles and small volcanos.

"And that's a city," Bishop explained as he changed the picture. "Those are buildings, places where the people of Earth live."

"No trees or caves?"

"No, we live in buildings on Earth. And considering what it costs to move nowadays," he added parenthetically, "we try to stay as long as we can."

"Stay? But why stay?" She found the concept more strange than the building itself. People moved or they died. "Do not reeka find you and eat you?"

"There are no reeka on Earth that eat men."

"No reeka?"

"Not a one like those you know," he answered, reacting to the delighted expression on her face. "We haven't had animals like reeka on Earth for a long, long time."

This was something she never dared hope would be possible: a world free of the giant saurians, a world where there was no cause to fear. "No reeka!" she exclaimed.

Her mind conjured up visions of her tribe during their constant flights from the flesh-eaters. She recalled how her people separated and ran off in small groups hoping to confuse the monstrous saurians so that some would be saved. All her life she had been hunted and that last horror-filled flight with Konu was still fresh in her memory. She remembered with vivid clarity how they rushed from tree to cave to tree in their attempt to avoid the death that sought them out no matter where they went. It was hard to live in a world where saurians ruled.

"In fact," said Gene, breaking into her memories, "about the only place on Earth you'll find wild animals is in the parks."

Another meaningless word! she thought. *There are so many today.* "Parks?" she inquired, wanting to digest the new term's meaning instantly. "What is parks?"

"A park," he explained, "is a large piece of land with a wall around it. It is away from the city." He pointed to the image on the screen again. "The parks are made to look like places where animals once lived. Trees and flowers and grass are planted in the parks. But we have no animals, so we go to other worlds, like yours, to get things to put in the parks."

"Parks," she said. Then she smiled again. But her mind kept dwelling upon a paradise where there were no monstrous beasts to hunt her down and eat her. "No reeka!" she said softly.

For a while Bishop continued to show more three-dimensional glimpses of his world: the sleek vehicles he called cars sped on the smooth ribbons of rock called roads; craft flew in the skies; the people wore incredible clothing and ornaments that made the blue uniforms of the crew dull by comparison. Every picture excited

Leea more. She wished she could be on Earth now to see and feel all these wonders.

When the show ended, Gene replaced the boxes. He put his hands on Leea's shoulders, sliding them down her arms to hold her hands. He liked to touch her and she enjoyed being touched. Looking into her eyes, he said, "Leea, I know why you fear reeka. But why do the eggs upset you?"

Her head turned toward the cubicle. Though the eggs were behind a wall, Leea acted as though she could see them. She shuddered. "Eggs reeka," she said, feeling a chill wriggle through her body. "Reeka kill. Reeka eat."

Gene shook his head. This damn me Tarzan, you Jane dialogue was frustrating, but it always came to that whenever the saurians were mentioned. She'd suddenly go elemental. "But what's wrong with the eggs?" he asked. "They can't hurt you."

"Eggs reeka."

"All right, so reeka are in the eggs. But tell me why you stand and wait for the reeka to eat you? Why don't you run?"

Gene had said strange things about time and space and flying past the stars. But they weren't nearly as strange as his question about how her people died. Had he not faced the reeka on the beach and in the river? Did he not know what they did to people? How they paralyzed the will and turned one's limbs to water.

"No one runs from reeka," she said firmly. "Not when they find you." Then she lowered her face against his chest. "One hides," she insisted, "and one cannot always hide."

She felt his hand under her chin; she looked into his eyes, and for a moment it was as if she saw a reeka. Her brain whirled, her muscles were weak . . . and then the feeling was gone.

"Tell me Leea," he said in the tone that made his people move fast, "what is it you fear? What do they do? Why don't your people band together and fight? Kill the reeka."

Was it possible that he was not aware? He couldn't be *that* stupid! "Cannot fight," she said at last. "Cannot kill. Cannot run." But she would never again be forced to run. Hugging Gene with all her strength, she murmured happily in his ear, "Earth! No reeka! And then, oddly, she shuddered. "But you bring reeka on ship. You must not! You must kill reeka in eggs. If they get out, they will eat us all."

CHAPTER 13

David Grimsby's professional life touched upon anthropology only peripherally. Nevertheless his interest in Leea was high, especially when he noted the speed with which she learned the language and customs of Earth. Such rapid assimilation of an alien culture was surprising. Either she was extraordinarily intelligent or extraordinarily adaptable, perhaps both.

He noted that Leea's knowledge increased on an exponential curve. Already the girl grasped some of the more subtle aspects of Earth's language, a feat no doubt aided by her uncanny ability to empathize with her instructors.

David now had little difficulty conversing with her. Mostly she asked questions and he answered them as best he could. Frequently, he had to smile over some questions that were firmly rooted in naiveté and ignorance.

"Do all Earth people dress like this?" she asked. She pointed at David and a crewman to emphasize her question. Clothing wasn't new to Leea but the styles and colors were strange, and she seemed preoccupied by this single aspect of Earth civilization. "Or do they dress like Cassandra when she is not working?"

Self-consciously, David glanced down at the drab jump suit that was his working uniform. He tried to explain the nature of uniforms and fashions, but was stymied by Leea's refusal to understand why Earthfolk would discard perfectly good clothing because of the season of the year. David sympathized, but he was relieved when she didn't pursue the idea of style and fashion any further. He predicted a conversational morass where he would sink without leaving a trace. It was better to leave her with the microfiche of magazines and newssheets and let her make her own dreams and decisions about underclothes and accessories.

There were still three ship-days of travel to go before breakout. Then, if all the navigational charting was correct, the freighter would emerge from Cth space near Earth's solar system. The tension hadn't yet built toward that wire-taut, nerve-snapping time that always marked the last few minutes in Cth, when all the navigation and calculation reached a climax. When Bishop and Leea entered the control room, David and his wife were observing the ship's movement in the astrogation tank. David could not escape the feeling that he had been hunted down; Leea was eyeing him with that eager, expectant look that accompanied a question session.

"Well, what is it this time?" he asked.

"David. . . ." she started.

"I'm afraid you're trapped again," Bishop said. "Leea's been bothering me with a question all morning. And if you don't answer it, there'll probably be no living with her the rest of the trip."

David smiled. "I expect it's another question you're not qualified to answer."

"Isn't it always?" answered Bishop. "I guess I'm a lousy explainer; or maybe Leea finds it simpler to absorb information by empathizing with the scientific mind."

"I wonder if I should feel insulted," mused Dian.

"Don't," replied the commander. "Just feel fortunate that you're not male. Leea's male-oriented. She'll ask a man much more readily than she'll ask a woman."

"Now I *do* feel insulted," Dian said.

"You two shouldn't make fun of Leea's nature," David said. He patted Leea reassuringly on the shoulder. "She delights in learning. Her trouble is that she attempts to condense all of her learning into an extremely short time span. But that's no reason not to help her, and I'll do what I can.

"All right, my dear, what is it this time?"

"On Erigon," she began, "there are few people. Always we are in danger. Always the reeka hunt us, and when they find us we cannot escape. Once there were many in my tribe, but now we are few. Gene says there are no reeka on Earth. Are there many people on Earth?"

Many? David thought. Yes, there were many. Some people said too many. But if the current Earth population were compared with that of the past century—he shrugged. Many was a relative term. There were about two and a half billion people on Earth, which was a goodly number, but hardly the billions that had swarmed the planet a century and a half ago. David wondered if he could make Leea understand, or if he would have to use the ancient words, "as many as the stars in the sky; as many as the pebbles on the beach." Two and a half billion was still a lot.

"Two hundred years ago," he said, "there were

over eight billion people on Earth. There were so many people that they pushed against each other. Everywhere there were people. It was impossible to get away from them. They swarmed like flies on a dead animal. They had no enemies except themselves. There were no reeka to hunt them and so the people hunted each other. Great bands called armies would fight and kill each other, but this did not reduce the number of the people, for no matter how many were killed, more were born. And finally the land became too small to hold them. They starved. They ate nearly all the animals. They even ate each other. It was a dreadful time."

Leea's face was blank with incomprehension.

David shrugged. "Forget it," he said. "There are many people on Earth. Many more than you have ever seen. But there are not as many as there were."

"Why not?" she asked.

"Because the tribes of men finally understood that if the numbers of people were not reduced, men would kill themselves by their very numbers. Do you understand this?"

"I think so," she replied, an answer that David was fairly sure meant she didn't understand at all. Leea was very human in certain aspects. He wondered how to proceed, and the silence grew between them. Suddenly Leea smiled. "Go on," she said. "I don't really understand you, but I may if you keep talking. Right now it doesn't make sense that there could be too many people."

"You didn't live on Earth during the past century," Grimsby explained. "It was a dreadful time. Finally the governments—the tribal councils—decided that families could not have more than one child."

"How could they stop them? Nobody can stop babies from coming."

"You have never heard of taxes, have you?" David asked.

Leea shook her head. "No. What are they?"

David laughed. "Do you know what money is?"

"No. Is it something to wear?"

David shrugged helplessly. "Until you learn what money is, I can't tell you about taxes, and until you learn what taxes are, you can't learn how we reduced our population. But you may remember that our tribes taxed couples heavily if they had more than one child, and people do not like to pay taxes. So they stopped having so many children; after a few hands of years the numbers of people were less. Believe me, Leea, on Earth the pocketbook is more important than sex."

"That is hard to believe," Leea said. "Only hunger and thirst are more important than sex on Erigon. Is this pocketbook something like hunger?"

"When it's empty it's exactly like hunger," David said. "But now let's learn something about money and taxes. You'd better know more about those things than you do or you'll be in trouble on Earth."

"Okay," Leea agreed. "You tell me. You show me. I learn."

David sighed and launched into a brief explanation of governments and finances and taxes. And Leea listened, nodding occasionally as she grasped what he was saying. Grimsby enjoyed teaching Leea, for she wanted to learn and worked desperately to understand. And, indeed, a large portion of the teachings stuck with her. She was a quick student all right, her memory was retentive and she could reason at a high level if she had enough data to work with. She quickly absorbed the idea of a medium of exchange and the advantages money had over a barter economy like the one in which she had been raised. David also enjoyed the way she smiled and sought more information as soon as she assimilated and organized data. She wouldn't be entirely at loose ends when she reached Earth.

"There isn't really much more," David said as he finished the story of the defused population explosion a few hours before breakout. "Soon," he said, "very soon, the poorer people were not so poor. They had less taxes and fewer mouths to feed. And Earth had fewer people using its resources and occupying space. Gradually the penalties for excess children grew harsher. Prison sentences and sterilization were added to fines and taxes for excess children. And Earth's population—once a threat to Man's existence—dropped from ten to less than three billion and, because of the eugenics laws, had improved as it had dropped. Successive generations were more intelligent, more socially conscious and more responsible, and finally the strict laws were no longer necessary. My world acquired something it had been sorely lacking in for quite some time—space and freedom."

"Space?" Leea said. "Who needs that? There is much space on Erigon. Plenty of space for both men and reeka. But the reeka search for us. Why do they do this?"

David shrugged. "I don't know," he said. "But we are not going to Erigon. We are going to Earth, and nowadays there is plenty of room for everyone. There is space to breathe, space to live comfortably, space to relax. We live today as people must have lived in those days before men learned how to fly. Now there is plenty of room for forests and animals, and we are trying to restore some of the extinct species by transferring similar animals from other worlds. Today there is ample room to build expensive and expansive tourist playgrounds like Africa-World, Asia-World and the new park we will call Dino-World."

"Tell me about the parks," Leea said, and David found himself in the midst of more explanations.

WHEN Leea finally decided she understood the gist of Grimsby's explanations it was time for breakout. The ship had moved into the area that the navigation computers said was close to Earth's solar system. Orders were issued; people took their stations. Navigational data were checked and rechecked as the ship approached breakout point. Slowly it descended through the Cth component and hung on the edge of normal spacetime. Tension built as the crew waited for the breakout. A lot of things had to be done quickly in the last split second that the ship remained in hyperspace. Leea and the Grimsbys stayed out of the way. At the moment they were useless and helpless as they watched the crew go through breakout drill.

When the time finally came, the ship lurched and shuddered, and suddenly the normal lights and colors of threespace and normal spacetime appeared around them. For the last time Gene Bishop presided over a smooth breakout. Off to the left glowed the golden brilliance of Sol, Earth's daystar. And within radio range was the Ceres beacon. It was a truly magnificent planetfall. The *J-17* was less than three days from touchdown on Earth.

THE landing was standard and uneventful, and the *J-17* came to vest some six months objective after her takeoff. It was superb pilotage and Leea glowed at the compliments the crew heaped on their captain. Everyone knew there was a lot of luck in a breakout so fantastically close to target, but luck was part of the mystique that surrounded a good skipper.

As the decontamination crews cleared the outside of the ship, the vision screens showed spaceport scenes and traffic. Everyone was anxiously waiting for the "all clear" when the locks would be opened and the crew could go through landing contamination. Leea was quivering with excitement, but she shook with no more eagerness than the rest of the crew. They were home.

David and Dian stood side by side looking at the screens, which showed stretches of gray airstrip lined with silvery craft gleaming in the light of Earth's single sun. In the distance stood the gaunt steel skeleton of a communications tower, and behind it were the hazy images of the spectacular metropolis that the Grimsbys called home—the city where David and Dian had an apartment; the city that held the Marshal Natural History Museum. They had a feeling of quiet pride. They had accomplished their mission: the dinosaur eggs were safely on Earth.

There was no ceremony awaiting them as they finally disembarked from the *J-17*, no dignitaries to greet their arrival. Spaceflight was routine nowadays. There was only the motor tram and its uniformed driver exchanging the usual small talk with them about what had happened since they had left. As the decon crews went through the spaceship, the occupants of the freighter were taken across the airstrip to the hospital where they were checked through an enormous diagnosticon and passed into the general hall.

A delegation from the Marshal Museum waited for David and Dian Grimsby; a number of sweethearts and relatives waited for the crew members; and a few reporters and TV cameramen from the local media stood nearby. The latter seemed more interested in the unexpected appearance of the red woman than David and Dian and the dinosaur eggs they had brought back with them.

CHAPTER 14

The first five days Gene Bishop spent on his home world were mostly devoted to preparing reports about the events of the voyage and his stay on Erigon. The former commander personally visited Jeff Chalfin's sister and attempted to tell her how her brother died; he didn't do too well. Bishop readjusted to civilian clothing; for though he was still in the employ of the government he was no longer a spaceship commander.

Leea was with him most of the time. How glorious she made those days! Bishop and Leea traveled as much as they could and Leea learned more about Earth from a neurosynthesizer. Finally they settled into a newly furnished apartment next to the Dino-World grounds, which were located a few hours by air from Spaceport City.

Their apartment was a luxury-class dwelling equipped with considerably more than the requirements for survival. As an executive, Bishop rated a house and an increase in salary. The dwelling had six spacious rooms, plus two bathrooms. There was a huge picture window overlooking the land that was being developed into the prehistoric animal park.

Leea still found it peculiar to see but one sun in Earth's sky. She and Bishop were standing at the picture window and gazing out at the bright world being manufactured before them—a world similar to Erigon in so many ways. The exhibit dwarfed all others. According to the information tapes provided by the government the completed park would cover a total of a thousand acres, and all of it was under Bishop's supervision.

There was little for Bishop to do during this phase of Dino-World's construction, except to watch the contractors change the shape of the earth. So he accepted the Grimsbys' invitation to bring Leea to the Marshal Laboratories for a visit. The dinosaur eggs were now incubating and it would be several weeks before they would hatch. David Grimsby thought it would be nice for the four of them to get together and make some plans for the future; neither David nor Dian was about to abandon the dinosaurs merely because they would be in a park.

It was a pleasant time and despite Bishop's protests, Leea became a ten-day wonder. Some video reporters from *Transworld* saw her on the streets of Spaceport City one day and ran a video feature on an alien's visit to Earth. Leea's image was projected via every visual medium at the newspeople's disposal, and as a result she appeared on several one-minute commercial spots that brought her a considerable income. Presently the oddity of her appearance became commonplace and her life returned to less hectic channels. Bishop sighed with relief, for though he knew it would ultimately happen, he had been afraid that it would last longer. But TV audiences were notoriously blasé, and in a few weeks Leea was able to stroll the streets without causing more than one or two heads to turn at the sight of her scarlet skin. This made Bishop particularly happy since he preferred to share Leea with no one, and especially not with a curious public.

THEY were back at Dino-World when David called them on the phone.

"Would you like to come to the research center?" David asked. "The eggs are about to hatch. There's movement in them."

"That's nice."

"And would you bring Leea?"

"I wouldn't go without her," Bishop said.

"Be here in two hours if you can," David said. He hung up leaving Bishop looking at a blank screen in puzzlement. Such abruptness was not like David.

The Marshal Research Center was forty-five kilometers south of Dino-World. It was built near the park for the convenience of scientists who wished to study the prehistoric fauna, but somehow the center had been finished long before serious work began on the park. Since Leea was afraid of the eggs, it took a bit of persuasion to get her to accompany him; when appeals to reason didn't work, authoritarianism did. Bishop was thankful that Leea had been raised in a male-dominant society; it solved a lot of his problems, although it created some he never suspected were involved in communal living.

Bishop's boots echoed on the marble floor of the main hall of the Marshal Center, barren except for a bronze, life-sized bust of the man who had founded the original museum back in the early 1900s, and a few bulletin boards announcing the foundation's latest activities. Every so often a man or woman wearing a white laboratory uniform or dull-green jump suit passed him as he crossed the hall and proceeded down the corridor. Beside him, Leea's footsteps were as quiet as his were noisy. He didn't have to ask anyone for directions to the incubator room. Leea moved toward it like a steel ball toward a magnet, and the VIP passes the Grimsbys had sent kept the security people off their backs. They went through the guarded door to the complex, and once inside Leea started shivering.

"Reeka!" she cried.

"They can't be more than babies," Bishop replied.

"They're still reeka and they're dangerous. They'll kill us if they can."

"Okay, so they'll kill us. Where are they?"

"Behind that door," Leea said, pointing to one of the featureless steel rectangles set in the masonry wall. Bishop pushed the door open and viewed the gaggle of white-coated personnel surrounding Dian and David. An enigmatic machine stood in the center. David smiled as he saw Bishop and the tension drained from his face.

"So glad you came, Gene. You too, Leea. Here, let me explain what's going on this afternoon."

"You don't have to," Leea said. "The reeka hatch. Soon this world will be like Erigon unless you kill them before they get too large."

The center of the chamber was dominated by the incubator. It had a hexagonal base, each side of which was approximately one meter in length. Above the base the hexagon was clear plastic, forming a six-sided chamber into which most of the people present were peering. Within the chamber lay the eggs from the mud of Erigon.

There was much more equipment in the room but most of it was meaningless to Bishop.

"This apparatus," said Dian Grimsby to Bishop, "duplicates the exact conditions of the beach at Erigon. I don't think we've forgotten a thing. We made conditions inside the chamber exactly the same. We even brought the mud in which they were laid. It's going to be a successful hatch. I can't see how we can fail under these controlled conditions." Her voice, however, was not as confident as her words.

"We've even duplicated the solar radiation of Erigon's suns," said David. "And we've kept sensors focused on the eggs. Our information indicates that the eggs contain living saurians—they should break through their shells any moment now."

"Oh, they'll hatch all right," Leea said. "And they'll grow very fast if you feed them well. When they're big enough, they'll eat you. Reeka always eat men."

David laughed. "They're not going to eat anybody. They'll be safe enough where we keep them. Stop worrying, and watch them hatch."

Leea shook her head, but she stayed with the group. As Dian checked the sensors focused on the eggs, Bishop began to share the excitement of the Grimsbys and the other scientists. "There's lots of movement inside," she said. "They ought to be coming out pretty soon."

An elongated yellow egg showed the first indications of movement. It wobbled a bit, then revealed a dark, jagged hole. The hole cracked along one edge, which spread to form a network of cracks that extended clear around the shell. Bishop could discern a tiny gray beak with a knob near its end. The beak continued to work at the shell until the cap dislodged and moved upward from the pressure exerted by the creature inside.

The animal's pale purple head pushed through the cracked shell. The head was rather long and its posterior end flared into the beginnings of a bony shield. A Ceratopsia, thought Bishop, recalling Grimsby's description. It was a tiny *Triceratops*. The horns were missing but those rudimentary bumps above the eyes and on the beak would develop into the formidable weapons of the adult saurian. Right now the potential giant was tiny and cute!

The baby dinosaur slowly crawled from the shell to bask in the warmth of the incubation machine. Strange, Bishop thought, how much difference infancy made. The little beast gave no indication that it would become a walking nightmare, a living tank capable of smashing through a building with its monstrous head.

More eggs cracked. And with every crack the scientists recorded the hatching data. It was even more strange, Bishop thought, that grown men and women should be so excited over an event that had probably occurred for millions of years without anyone paying a great deal of attention to it. After the first few, Bishop's interest in hatching dinosaurs quickly palled; after the sixth egg, he was satisfied that things would continue without a hitch. Leea was becoming increasingly nervous, and as the seventh egg's ankylosaur wriggled free of its ovoid prison, Bishop was satisfied that his park would have an adequate number of inhabitants.

"I think I've seen enough of this maternity ward to hold me," he said.

"Let's go home," Leea said. "Let's leave these reeka."

"Fascinating," breathed David, apparently not even hearing Bishop's words, "truly fascinating!" His attention was riveted on the hatching eggs.

"Yes," said Bishop. "But we're going back to the house."

Dian heard him and turned away from the hatching eggs long enough to look at him. "Can't you stay a while longer—at least until we've hatched all the eggs? We haven't gotten our first sauropod yet."

"You see one dinosaur hatch, you've seen them all," Bishop chuckled. "I've had enough. I'm confident that your incubator will do an excellent job and that all the dinosaurs will appear on schedule. But they give Leea screaming fits and there's no reason to prolong her agony. Just look at her."

"I understand," Dian said as she looked at Leea's set face.

"I think I'd better take her on a tour through the park, because once those animals start prowling about its hills and jungles, she'll never come close to it."

"It's too bad she has these horrid delusions about the saurians," Dian said.

"Possibly you'd have different ideas about them if they'd eaten *your* relatives," Bishop said.

Leea didn't say anything. She simply left the room, and after a moment, Bishop followed.

CHAPTER 15

In the six months that followed the hatching of the Erigon saurians, Earth's technology and nature combined to prepare Dino-World for an eager public. The physical refinements of terra-forming the landscape with Erigon were accomplished with startling rapidity. The plants were force-grown, the coldsleep animals were thawed, checked and released, and the saurians placed in forced-growth chambers. As quickly as skill and technology could do the job, the area was prepared for occupancy by its ruling class. Human and robot laborers toiled tirelessly to make Dino-World a masterpiece, a convincing true-to-life microcosm of Erigon, balanced ecologically with transplanted fauna and flora that simulated the Mesozoic. The process impressed Bishop who, although well acquainted with the science of his day, was still amazed by its practical applications.

As curator, he oversaw the construction and made suggestions to bring the environment into line with what he had seen and recorded on Erigon.

Dino-World's magnificent cliffs rose jaggedly into the sky, then receded into the distance. The skyscraping formations had been created with enough caves and boltholes to please the most demanding ecologists, who sought accuracy in the terrain of this artificial world as well as safe shelters. Many smaller animals would need protection from the larger predators.

It was, in a way, a cruel world they were building, but nature is never kind, and from a teaching standpoint accuracy and honesty were thought to be more valuable than sentimentality. Therefore, Dino-World lacked some of the candy coating that characterized Africa-World, where all the flesh eaters were surreptitiously fed so they wouldn't bother the herbivorous wildlife.

The forests and jungles that grew in lush abundance were partly composed of contemporary trees, and partly of those from the Mesozoic world of Erigon. There were tree ferns, pines, cycads, ginkgos and others that blended into one unending haze of green in the distance. There was a winding river and lakes large enough to support even the most gigantic of the marsh grazers. And while initially there would have to be tons of synthetic and prepared foods, in time, if everything went right the area would be fifty percent self-supporting.

In all, as Bishop gazed across the wastes and jungles of Dino-World, there seemed little that was incongruous.

The Grimsbys, who practically lived at the project, agreed with him. Of course there were the modern security towers that enclosed the acreage. Their purpose was blatantly obvious, but the eye passed over these samples of twenty-second century technology and focused on the world inside. The engineers and terraformers who had designed the park had done a good job. It would contain all the life placed inside it and keep out all the life of the outside world. No herds of dinosaurs would go charging through Earth's city streets.

There were incongruities other than the security towers that revealed Dino-World's modernity. A curving length of monorail, supported on towering ferroconcrete legs, snaked throughout most of the park. This track would transport the visitors to Dino-World on a safe ride into antiquity. The supports were constructed to keep the trains well above the heads of even the largest carnosaurs. Equally tall towers held the numerous video cameras that would record every moment within the portion of park that was accessible to visitors. The pictures were relayed to the control tower, which was beside Gene and Leea's home.

The northern area of Dino-World was beyond the range of either monorail or videotape cameras. A two-hundred-hectare plot, still unfinished, lay behind a ridge of cliffs awaiting the hatching of more dinosaurs and the needs of future expansion. The area was desolate and barren of vegetation. Gene flippantly christened it Desolation World. It was a relic of the old world after the Last War, a harsh, lifeless desert terrain that was in marked contrast to the lush growth in the recreation area.

David and Dian supervised the growth of their dinosaurs in specially prepared yards that had been erected outside the Marshal Center. The dinosaurs grew rapidly and required an enormous amount of food, but their needs had been foreseen and were adequately supplied. Though the Grimsbys and other paleontologists still argued over the growth rate of Earth's extinct dinosaurs, none of them thought their growth would be as rapid as these from Erigon. Noticeable growth had occurred within three days of hatching, and the growth continued on an exponential curve. Within five weeks the creatures were as large as big dogs, and when park construction finally terminated they were half their adult size. At this time they were immobilized with tranquilizers and transported to their habitat. A year after their return to Earth the dinosaurs' growth tapered off, and they were what David and Dian estimated to be adults except for trifling additions in bulk that time would give. They were about as big as they would get. After all, the cubic dimensions of a 40 ton brontosaur were not much greater than those of a 20 tonner.

The full-grown reptiles roamed the rugged terrain, the herbivores subsisting on the abundant vegetation and the carnivores upon the rapidly multiplying mammals that were bred at other wildlife preserves and turned loose in Dino-World. As the Grimsbys expected, the flesh-eating dinosaurs maintained their aversion to eating other saurians, and the tranquility that Bishop had wondered about settled over this artificial world.

Everything was ready for the grand opening, which had been set for the next month. Advertisements had been on television for weeks—tiny spot ads that would blossom to full flower as the moment of opening arrived. David and Dian were constant visitors and made frequent tours of the park on the monorail system. The silvery trains consisted of articulated open cars, each bearing a colorful picture of an Erigonian dinosaur. The trains were each headed by a car with a conical nose. Each car had its own drive wheels, and trains could be virtually any size by adding or removing cars. The tracks wove through approximately two-thirds of the park, avoiding the area of Desolation-World. The monorail curved between the trees, around the bases of towering cliffs and above the artificial streams and lakes. All of the trains' travels were transmitted by video cameras to the control tower, where they would be monitored in case of an accident or malfunction. After all, beasts the size of these Erigonian horrors could be dangerous.

David, Dian and Gene Bishop sat in the front car of a short train and moved across the Mesozoic terrain with its planted jungle. Some of the big saurians were visible and seemed to be at home in their new surroundings. A trio of magenta-skinned Ceratopsia, all resembling the *Triceratops*, were testing the electronic security fence and recoiling from the charged nets that hung from the towers. A carnosaur munched on the body of a large deerlike mammal. Two marsh dwellers lifted their tiny heads on long necks and gazed curiously at the train. The general scene was a satisfactory imitation of Earth's Mesozoic era.

The public, Bishop thought, would be satisfied. A *Ceratopsia* and an *Ankylosaurus* below the train lifted their heavy heads to observe the cars as they moved overhead and passed beyond the planted jungle and across a wide and verdant plain. A grazing stegosaur looked incuriously at them for a moment and resumed eating.

"It's a pity Leea wouldn't come along for this

ride," said David, craning his neck for a better look at a distant carnosaur striding rapidly across the plain. "I think we did a good job here, one to be proud of, and it's as peaceful as a church."

"You want to show off for your pupil," said Dian.

"I haven't been able to get her inside this park since the first trip," Bishop said. "That contact with the saurians was strong when they were eggs, and you can imagine how powerful it is now. Believe me, nothing is going to get her on these grounds."

Some hundred meters from the passing monorail, a theropod roared. Its scaly head turned to watch the gleaming conveyance, even as the monster's image faded into the background. Dian had to speak louder as the animal roared again.

"You can't blame the girl," she said. "Her entire life has been spent living in terror of these creatures. You can't expect her to flee one world of violence and freely enter another, particularly when the world outside has none of these nightmare creatures."

"Ah—so you think they're nightmares, too," Bishop said.

Dian shook her head. "No. To me they're fascinating; to Leea they're nightmares. I was empathizing."

"I've tried to dispel her fears," Bishop said. He eyed Dian closely for a moment and then continued speaking. "I've tried to tell her about all the safety features we've installed here at Dino-World. I told her that the monorail is too high for even the tallest flesh-eating reekas to reach.

And I described the towers and the nets that could electrocute the biggest elephant in Africa-World. It did no good, even with the knowledge she's already assimilated. She just won't enter this park now the lizards are here."

"Nevertheless," said David, "we should be satisfied with Leea. She's learned more in the brief time she's been with us than I ever expected. She's quite at home on Earth."

For a moment Bishop beamed. David recalled how he reacted to Leea when he had brought her aboard the starship. Even then Bishop was considerate. Prior to Leea, he was the typical frozen-faced disciplinarian. Even the relationship with Cassandra was a by-the-numbers affair. But that passed with Leea's arrival and once the freighter lifted from the rugged terrain of Erigon, Bishop seemed to exist as much for Leea as for the command of his ship. His personality had become more human and less authoritarian; and almost in ratio with his increasing humanity came a decrease in the confidence the crew had in him. No wonder the government demanded unmarried spacemen and women. Marriage could louse up the efficiency of a crew to such an extent that the ship might be destroyed. But on the whole, Bishop was a far more pleasant personality now than he had been prior to Leea's arrival.

"The way Leea learns reminds me of the way our dinosaurs grew," remarked Dian.

"Oh?" asked Bishop.

"Both processes occurred with a rapidity none of us ever predicted. How fortunate it has been for all of us. Now Leea can talk and tell us about human life on Erigon. As for the dinosaurs well, they're already big enough to please anyone."

"They grew fast enough," Bishop said. "Too fast, maybe. I never dreamed they'd reach adult size so quickly."

"Horses grow almost as fast," Dian said.

"Elephants don't," Bishop said.

"Different worlds, different growth. What we call elephants today aren't the same animals that were on Earth before the Last War. They're not native."

"Neither are the dinosaurs."

"So what's your point?" Dian asked.

"Remember the day on Erigon when I made the crack about the pacifist dinosaurs?"

David remembered the feeble battle that began almost immediately after Bishop's comment. "So?"

"When I made that remark I was specifically referring to Dino-World and the disappointed customers who'd expect to see some action for their money. And right then—on cue—we got the kind of action that would make customers squeal, but wouldn't hurt the saurians. The beasts put on a show for us."

"They don't have enough brains," David said. "You know that."

"All right," continued Bishop, "so they don't have brains. Maybe they've got something else. It's fairly obvious they have some built-in control over the humanoids and mammals on Erigon. The carnosaurs, big and clumsy as they are, catch all the mammals they need to keep them alive. They still do; only now the mammals they catch are not native to Erigon. I think we should consider the possibility that we're dealing with something more than a food-gathering adaptation. The dinosaurs have something more sophisticated than we want to admit."

"You mean like hypnosis?" asked Dian. "Can you believe that one of these stupid beasts can dominate the will of an intelligent organism? Such speculation is outrageous, Gene. Really! You're implying that the saurians have a mental capacity equal to or greater than ours. These dinosaurs are like the ones that once lived on Earth; their skulls are mostly bone—with very little room for brain. And we know that Leea's brain is fully as developed as our own."

"Maybe brains aren't the answer," said Bishop. "I know some pretty stupid stage magicians who are pretty good hypnotists."

"Then just what are we talking about?" asked Dian.

"Hypnotism? Communion? Community thought? Mass mind? Telepathy? Oh, I can offer lots of speculation, but all I know is that there is something truly alien about those saurians. My imagination has been running wild lately, and one of the thoughts that keeps me up at night is that those dinosaurs fought on cue because they somehow knew that what was what we wanted."

"Gene!" David remonstrated.

"They knew," Bishop insisted. His voice was flat. "Somehow I can't get rid of the idea that they knew and for some reason they didn't want to disappoint us. I think they wanted us to believe they were precisely the kind of creatures we wanted. Their flesh-eaters blew it with Leea and Chalfin, but the idea was good enough to get their eggs brought to Earth. Now for the big question—why did they want us to take their eggs to Earth?"

"Gene, you're as bad as Leea," Dian said.

"I live with the girl, and she's smart," Bishop said.

"Your idea is mind-boggling," David said. "If you *are* right, there is only one conclusion we can draw: those beasts are highly intelligent."

"Oh David!" Dian said reproachfully.

"They could have wanted to be brought to Earth," David said.

"Why?" asked his wife.

"We've talked that over before. Their age distribution on Erigon is all wrong. There were too many adults compared to juveniles and too few adults in proportion to the planetary area. I think they're dying out, and if Bishop is right, they know it!"

"Preposterous!" exclaimed Dian. "But granting the possibility that such an outlandish theory is true, why would they come to Earth?"

"To get away from what was killing them on Erigon," replied Bishop. "And here's some more food for thought. Remember when we rescued Leea? Something happened to me on that riverbank. There was something about that saurian's eyes that made me feel dizzy when it looked at me. I had to fight to stay alert."

"Hypnosis taking effect?" ventured David not really knowing if he believed his own words.

"You said a bond probably existed between the

saurians and their prey," said Bishop. "Couldn't it be that we were also prey? And remember that hydrofoil incident with the plesiosaur when Chalfin was killed? Before the carnosaur died it gazed out over the water."

"The water——" David began.

Bishop interrupted, "That's right. And it was *then* that the plesiosaur attacked. *Only* then! The saurian could have attacked before; we saw it swimming about before we ever saw the carnosaur or Leea on the beach. But it waited until. . . ."

David's mind was racing. The implications staggered him. "If what you say is fact, you have discovered something that's truly frightening. Man cannot tolerate a species more able than himself, at least not on his home planet. And we've brought these beasts here. I hope to God you're wrong."

"So do I. I don't know what to do with the idea, and somehow it won't go away. Do you have any suggestions about what we might do?"

David shook his head.

Bishop paused. Then he said, "It might be better to close the park, stop it from opening to the public until we can flush out the truth."

"But you can't do that," said Dian. "You can't close a government park—especially one that the public has been waiting for—just because *nothing* has happened."

And nothing had happened, Bishop thought— not yet.

"There seems to be no alternative," David said. "We'll have to open Dino-World as scheduled and keep a constant watch from the control tower."

"I suppose that's the best we can do," said Bishop. "But at the first sign of anything wrong, I'm going to close the place and call in the armed forces."

As the monorail returned to the boarding platform, the implications of his discussion with Bishop worried Grimsby. He stepped from the car and extended his hand to Dian, conscious of an odd feeling of uneasiness. In the distance he could hear the grumblings of the saurians. There was always a certain amount of background noise among the big lizards. In some ways, he thought with faint amusement, they were much like chickens and ducks making small noises as they fed. But this was different; a couple of carnosaurs and a gaggle of sauropods congregated in one of the nearby meadows. A huge *Tyrannosaurus* appeared to have taken over the central spot of the conclave. It was a gaudy beast with an over-abundance of yellow stripes marking its slate-gray hide; these gleamed golden in the sunlight as the creature towered over the other beasts. It was making aggressive-sounding noises, but neither it nor the others made any hostile moves.

"The Chairman of the Board is telling the members off," David remarked with a wry smile. "I wonder what he has on his mind."

"Whatever it is," Dian said. "It must be unpleasant, judging from the noise. There's a lot of roaring going on down there." And indeed, it sounded like the prelude to battle. The big *Tyrannosaurus* bellowed and rose to its full height; the great jaws clashed; the fangs gleamed; the huge body quivered as great muscles bulged beneath its striped hide. Then it stalked off leaving the others to grumble and squeak and groan. "Do you think they communicate?" Dian asked as she watched the great beast vanish into a nearby clump of trees. "Their attitudes were a lot like those of a committee. I can't help being struck by the similarity."

David laughed. "Next thing you know, we'll be speculating on whether they have a philosophy."

"Don't laugh, David. We don't know much about these animals."

"That wasn't why I laughed. It was the ridiculous thought of a board of directors composed of dinosaurs that tickled me. I couldn't help thinking of that pelvic region, and all the puns about saving afterthoughts."

Dian chuckled.

> When faced with problems too severe
> Its head would ache from ear to ear
> And since its ends were so related
> Its rearward end got constipated.

David laughed at the mental picture of the frustrated saurian, but mixed with the amusement was a tiny cold thread of worry that squiggled down his spine. Dian was right. That group did look like a committee. After all, he should recognize committees, he'd been on enough of them. And the *Tyrannosaurus* looked like a disgruntled minority of one. He shrugged. This was a stupid sort of speculation. But there was something queer about these Erigonian lizards. Their habit patterns weren't at all what one would expect.

David grasped his wife's hand and began walking rapidly toward the exit.

"What's the rush?" Dian asked.

"I want to get home," he said as he hurried toward their car. "There's something I want to check, and I want to do it right now."

"You're acting like a boor," Dian said.

"So what? Gene understands. We'll be forgiven." He led her to the car and drove off toward the research center, leaving Bishop standing on the platform with a mildly startled expression on his face. Bishop hadn't been following their conversation. He was immersed in speculations of his own, and their abrupt departure caught him unprepared. He watched the Grimsbys' car scoot through the main gate and out onto the highway. He shrugged. Scientists were a strange lot, he decided, and paleontologists were stranger than most.

He turned and looked out over the expanse of Dino-World. The big *Tyrannosaurus* had come closer to the boarding platform. It stood about a hundred meters away, outside the protective screen that kept the beasts away from the platform, and it was looking at him.

He felt a sudden chill. Abruptly he turned and walked down the ramp toward his quarters.

CHAPTER 16

Dino-World opened to the public on schedule, and the apprehensions of both Bishop and the Grimsbys were drowned in the rush of visitors. Bishop still had reservations about the harmlessness of the dinosaurs and the security of the park was uppermost in his mind. He checked men and machinery continuously, looking for possible weaknesses and finding none. Still, his sleep was filled with nightmares in which the gigantic saurians suddenly broke security and raged through crowds of visitors, gobbling them up in a bloody, orgiastic feast. If it hadn't been for Leea, his life would have been worse; she seemed to understand his worries and, with her marvelous empathy, managed to keep him reasonably calm. But the pressure was always there, and Bishop became increasingly conscious of the responsibility of his post and of the almost criminal carelessness of the visitors who every day took liberties with security that made him shudder. If any of these beasts were like the one that had attacked Leea on Erigon, there would inevitably be casualties.

So he tightened security, increased the strength of the fences and prayed that some inquisitive fool wouldn't find a way to get into an eyeball to eyeball confrontation with a carnosaur. Being a park curator wasn't the blissful existence he had anticipated. But he couldn't return to space and abandon Leea. He was caught in an insoluble dilemma. Leea was aware of this and did her best to make his life more pleasant, but there were nights when Bishop lay awake remembering adventures on other worlds. Space had infected his blood and shaped his soul. Not even a perfect wife and a secure job compensated for the lost ecstasy of traveling through the void.

His feelings were probably stimulated by his dislike of the saurians and Leea's fear and loathing of them. Her feelings about the reeka never changed. She wanted nothing to do with them. She wouldn't look at them, and once she discovered that nothing she could do would change the march of events, she did her best to ignore their existence.

Dino-World drew more patrons than anyone had predicted. People formed lines every day the park was open. Some even snuggled into the dinosaur-shaped topiaries that had been set outside the park's main gates and spent the night waiting for the gates to open. The trains were always filled to capacity and ran on a tight schedule from opening to closing hours. It was surprising how much interest was generated in the Mesozoic restoration. If business were maintained at this pace, the rest of the park area would soon have to be developed and opened to the public.

People craved wildlife parks. The artificial creations like Disneyparks had withered and died as people lost interest in mechanisms and robotics became commonplace. No one bothered to look at robot humans and animals. What people craved now were real, living animals—and the animal parks were economical enough that the public's wishes could be satisfied at profit to the treasury.

Bishop was called on regularly to visit ecology

groups and make speeches to civic organizations. Leea went with him on these trips, and on the rare times he was forced to talk at Dino-World Leea would go into the control tower and give him moral support. Although they were part of the job, Bishop hated speeches and he was always happy when they were over. Unfortunately, they were effective sales talks and the numbers of visitors at Dino-World were increased proportionally to the numbers of speeches. A business-oriented government could hardly be blamed for insisting that he help improve the gate receipts. The computerized sales and ticket reports were mute evidence of Bishop's ability as a salesman, and while he thought the tales of his adventures on Erigon and other worlds were sophomoric, they had a remarkable effect on people.

The silver monorail trains wound through the terraformed park. Children pointed and shrieked at the sight of the saurians, who were unimpressed by the humans. There were no real difficulties, and even the idiots who attempted to roam the park on foot were caught before they could be eaten The big *Tyrannosaurus* was a constant attraction as it always seemed to be bellowing and screaming at other lizards. But the threatened violence never materialized, although thousands of people thought it might and came back again and again in the hope they would be there when it did.

WEEKS passed during which nothing out of the ordinary occurred, but Bishop noticed that the big *Tyrannosaurus* had increased its vehemence and apparent anger at the others. Somewhere along the line Bishop started calling the monster *Oedipus rex*, to distinguish it from the others.

Slowly the beasts began to develop habit patterns.

Bishop found it impossible to follow their actions on the monitor screens after the sun went down, for with darkness all the behemoths would lumber out of camera range and disappear in the direction of the barren area known as Desolation World. He didn't think much of it; after all, even dinosaurs ought to have some privacy while they slept.

Once the park was closed for the night and the security guards and robots had taken over, Bishop would go to his quarters and join Leea. Sometimes there were visitors and the Grimsbys dropped in regularly. It was a nice, comfortable life without excitement—and it didn't sit well with Bishop. The Grimsbys were a welcome relief, despite the fact that their visits usually produced lengthy technical discussions about dinosaurs and Dino-World and worries about the safety of the patrons.

The nightmares were slow in coming. As the days passed they increased in frequency and horror, always involving dinosaurs. The principal figure became *Oedipus rex*. Always, Oedipus would come stalking out of a misty background and always Bishop would flee. There was no violence, no fear of being eaten, only the ultimate horror of that great scaly body chasing him across an endless succession of meadows and swamps.

Invariably he would awaken with a vicious head-ache, drenched with sweat and shivering uncon-trollably. That was when he needed Leea most—and she was always there.

He began to dread slumber, but couldn't stay awake forever. He had to talk with someone other than Leea. And so, one night when the Grimsbys were visiting, he told his experiences to David and Dian.

"You know, you may not be having night-mares," David said when Bishop finished. There was a sobriety about the paleontologist—a grim-ness—that Bishop hadn't seen before. Gone was the wide-eyed enthusiasm he had displayed on Erigon and in the Marshal Laboratories. His face was lined with evidence of work and fatigue.

"David has been putting in more hours lately than he ever did before in his life," remarked Dian. "It seems as if every time I look at him he's writing something or putting figures on paper. I've tried to get him to rest but I can't influence the man."

"Oh?" queried Bishop. "I thought the two of you always worked together."

David seemed not to hear while a slightly embarrassed look swept across his wife's face.

"We have," said Dian. "Until recently. David has taken it upon himself to—"

"You'd better let me explain it, dear," David interrupted. "I'll be frank with you, Gene. I haven't been able to sleep well myself of late. And it's not because I'm haunted by carnosaurs."

"Then what?"

"I suppose I've been feeling guilty."

"Guilty?" said Leea. "But why should you feel guilty? You're a good and kind man. Never have I known you to harm anyone."

Rising from his chair, David walked to the picture window. His back was to the group as he looked out toward the park and the illuminated regions of the preserve.

"Leea," he said, "your beauty transcends the physical. Like Dian, you fail to see the ugliness that can exist inside another person."

"Ugliness?" asked Leea. "The reeka are ugly. You are not."

"It's not that kind of ugliness," said David. "It's the ugliness that will sacrifice life in the pursuit of knowledge."

"Listen, David, if you're trying to assume blame for Chalfin's death, forget it. You're not responsible. That tragedy was no one's fault."

David turned a grim face toward Bishop. "I don't lose sleep over Chalfin," he said. "It's more than that. If I hadn't been instrumental in convincing the foundation to pursue the Erigon mission, I would sleep better."

"But. . . ."

"And if I hadn't been so hot to bring those eggs back to Earth, I wouldn't be worrying now. I should have been suspicious. The moment I saw those five saurians on Erigon that acted so strangely I should have asked you to terminate the mission and take us back to Earth."

"That wouldn't have been possible," insisted Bishop. "Even though the Marshal Foundation sponsored the expedition, it was still government-funded. We couldn't terminate unless there was a clear and present danger to human life."

"There was," David said, "only we didn't realize it."

In one graceful movement, Leea arose from her chair and crossed the room to where David was standing. She looked into his eyes and gently squeezed his hands.

"There is no evil in you," she said softly. "If there were, I would know. Nor could you have known what every person born on Erigon knows. I could not tell you, and Gene does not yet understand."

"That's simple for you to say, Leea, but it's not so simple for me to accept."

"There was good in your coming," Leea said, "for I am here with Gene. And had you not come to Erigon I would be dead."

"That's true," David said, "and it makes me feel better. But there are other things to be considered." He turned to Bishop. "I said that you might not be suffering from just ordinary nightmares. I meant that, Gene. There is something uncanny about the mentality of these saurians. And lately I've come to believe that this power they have over their victims is something far more than simple hypnotism."

"David thinks that the saurians are truly intelligent," said Dian, "despite their tiny brains."

"I've been checking the tapes, films and other data," David went on, "and it's all strongly indicative, but there comes a point when one has to go beyond paperwork. That's why I'm here tonight."

"You want more discussion?" Bishop inquired.

David shook his head. "I don't want to talk, Gene, I want to test my hypothesis."

"Meaning?"

"I want access to the control tower," said David. "I want to watch those screens. I think something is rotten in Dino-World."

"But David," exclaimed Bishop, thinking of the desolate area of the park into which the dinosaurs vanished every night, "you'd be sitting by those screens all night with nothing to see. The lizards go into Desolation World and that's beyond camera range."

"I know," said David. "But it's my time and my idea. All I ask is that you let me check my hypothesis. If there *is* something out of the ordinary, I can place my findings before the park bureau; I have some influence there. They respect my opinions."

Bishop could see no harm in David's request. If the man wanted to waste a perfectly good evening in the control tower, that was his concern.

"All right. I'll clear you with security."

"Thanks," sighed David.

Dian looked stricken but she said nothing, and after Bishop had made the necessary calls, she left with David to ascend the control tower above the boarding platforms of the monorail station. An hour elapsed, during which Bishop and Leea relaxed before their stereovision, sipping drinks and finishing some of the refreshments intended for their guests. Suddenly Leea scrambled to her feet. A look of utter horror appeared on her face.

She clutched Bishop's arm, "David . . . David is in danger!"

Bishop had learned some time ago that Leea's intuition was to be heeded. He didn't wait. He ran out of the house to the control tower ramp, followed by Leea.

"Dian!" he shouted as he burst into control room. Dian was crying hysterically and staring with wide eyes at one of the monitor screens. The screen was bright but the image was no longer there; it was as though the transmitting camera no longer existed. And David wasn't in the tower.

"Dian," said Bishop. "Where's David?"

The woman turned, tears streaming down her face, "Oh, Gene," she began, and her lip quivered. "David . . . is out there—and the dinosaurs are back. They attacked him!"

CHAPTER 17

David Grimsby was in the control tower only a few minutes after leaving the Bishop apartment. He had switched on the monitor screens and was looking at the prehistoric landscape—a vast tranquil area devoid of saurians.

"I'm going out there," he said. "I must contact those creatures!"

"What?" exclaimed Dian Grimsby. "You can't be serious!"

David nodded. "Deadly serious."

"Why didn't you mention this when we were downstairs?"

"That should be obvious," said David. His eyes continued to search the screen, looking for the slightest movement that would indicate the presence of dinosaurs. He found nothing.

Dian clutched David's arm. He could feel her tremble and could hear the fear in her voice. "You were afraid Gene wouldn't let you do anything as foolish as this. Come on, David—you're a scientist. We both are. You're too old to entertain such adolescent thoughts."

David shrugged. There was no use in trying to tell Dian just what he felt. He'd tried before. His spirit was heavy with dread of disaster to come and she couldn't see it.

"I'm sorry, Dian," he said gently, "but the only way I can do what I must is to go out there and test my idea."

"I can't let you! You're insane to go out there alone at night."

With a forced smile on his lined face, David

turned away from the monitors. "It won't be so bad. There's little danger. Remember Dino-World's safety precautions. There'll be no trouble."

"At least let me go with you," pleaded Dian.

David shook his head. "I need you here to watch the screens and go for help if I need it."

As Dian hesitated David smiled, knowing his reasoning was cogent enough to keep her in the tower. And to augment his words, he walked across the room and pressed a button on a wall panel. The panel slid open, revealing a storage rack that held blast rifles and hand blasters.

"Here's a little more insurance," he said, removing a blast rifle.

"You're not a good marksman," Dian reminded him as she gazed at the weapon. "I've seen you try to shoot those things."

"I might frighten them off," David said. "But don't worry, they won't bother me."

"I can't talk you out of this?" she asked.

David did not reply, nor was there any need. They understood each other. Their rapport, not as sophisticated as that between Leea and the saurians, was nevertheless extremely close. He was determined to go and she would not stop him.

David kissed his wife more lovingly than usual and left her watching the monitor screens. He went down to the boarding platform, and silently took a seat in the front car of the leading monorail train. He looked into the scanning camera, waved to his wife, and moved the throttle forward. The train moved silently from the platform and wound through the darkness of the shadowed green realm, partly illuminated by the lights along the track.

Presently he was on the curving track that faced the entrance to the desolate area. There he brought the train to a stop and stood in the shadowed car to face the blackness of Desolation World. His nostrils were filled with night odors. A cool breeze chilled his skin as he rested the rifle against the inside wall of the car. Almost mystically, the paleontologist brought his fingers to his temples, pressing them firmly against his skin, concentrating, attempting to send thoughts toward the hidden dinosaur retreat.

He stood there for half an hour, until he quivered with weariness. Nothing happened. Momentarily, his eyes glimpsed the white three-quarter moon that shone above the distant hills. He wondered if he were wrong. Once again he projected his thoughts:

You don't have to maintain the pretext any longer. You can show your true selves. I know you're not mindless lizards. I know you are intelligent.

And as David concentrated, his eyes detected movement from the shadowy depths of Desolation World. Shapes were slowly emerging from the darkness—awesome shapes, six of them, silhouetted in the light of the waxing moon.

That's it! I won't harm you. All I want is to communicate. We have so much to learn from each other.

They came out of the dark and into the beams of the park spotlights, their scaly hides gleaming in the light from the monorail tower. Each suborder was represented. The animals were a delegation.

The six behemoths halted in a semicircle around

the train. A gray *Tyrannosaurus*, somewhat smaller than the disagreeable brute Bishop called *Oedipus rex*, shifted its head from side to side, its eyes scanning every one of its five saurian companions. They turned their heads toward David.

David felt a chill as their bright gaze converged on him and the carnosaur bellowed. His theory *had* to be right! Once again, he pressed his temples: *Communicate. I know you can.*

The *Tyrannosaurus's* head lifted, slime oozing from its slightly open mouth. The lower jaws, teeth showing sharp and huge in the moonbeams, reached upward. Then the saurian snapped at the front car of the train.

David wasn't sure that the snapping was an aggressive act. He didn't want to move until his theory had been proven. Besides he was safe enough here in the train.

Speak to me . . . I know you can! Use the power that lets you dominate the minds of others on your home world. Speak to me!

The dinosaurs exchanged what David thought were puzzled looks, though they did not speak to him. But slowly, they turned their attention back to the train.

The brontosaur was the first to act, opening its mouth and bringing its awesome bulk to a point directly beneath the unmoving train. The serpentine neck swayed, stretched, and the jaws snapped at the car, crashing against the aluminum siding.

In one heart pounding instant, David forced himself to remain where he was, forced his automatic responses down. He wouldn't jump to escape those jaws . . . he wouldn't!

The brontosaur smashed its mighty jaws into the aluminum siding again, and the train rocked with the impact.

David reached automatically for the blast rifle, his eyes darting instantly to the monitor microphone. "Dian!" he started urgently. "They're hostile! I'm coming back!"

He reached for the throttle, but the *Brontosaurus* snapped again. There was the grating screech of saurian jaws raking metal and a snap as the man-made material began to give way.

The *Brontosaurus* was not alone now. As David realized the train wasn't moving, he saw a *Triceratops* and the armored monster that resembled an *Ankylosaurus* joining the *Brontosaurus*, as eager to destroy him, as capable of doing so. The *Triceratops* charged, ramming its armored head into the monorail support beneath the train, sending waves of force through the structure and almost toppling David where he stood, still trying frantically to get the battered train to move. Then the *Ankylosaurus* crashed its massive tail against the next support and the rail creaked, swayed even more. Sparks hissed from the drives, and the train still did not move . . . could not!

He clutched at the sides of the car, calling out to the monitor microphone in the hopes that Dian would hear him, but he knew the mechanism was smashed. He turned his attentions back to the dinosaurs, again sending frantic thoughts. . . .

I mean you no harm! I want to communicate. . . .

His thoughts were garbled, jumbled by the horror he felt. The supports cracked then, snapping like so much bamboo as the *Brontosaurus* smashed its side against the pillar. The section of the structure swayed gently from side to side as if caught in a gentle breeze, then picked up speed as the creature continued to smash from below, and each terrific impact brought the construction closer to total collapse.

As the *Ankylosaurus* once again whipped its mighty tail about, the lead car screeching and unable to withstand the pressure any longer, slowly rolled over the edge of the destroyed section of track and crashed to the ground.

The grate and clang of the remaining cars landing and ricochetting off the first added even more noise, but in seconds the last car had fallen and the echoes slowly died away.

David felt pain, excruciating pain, and tried to move his legs, realizing only then that he was trapped in the mangled, twisted wreckage. The side of the car he'd been standing in had crumpled like a piece of paper, crushing his legs between the two sheets of metal.

The pain increased when he tried to move, and a red haze settled over his eyes, rising only when he ceased his desperate efforts to free himself. He became aware, slowly, that in his terror he had gripped the blast rifle, and even now, after the tremendous fall from the top of the track, he still held it tightly in his hands.

He tried to move again, felt the pain in his legs and screamed in agony.

And heard a grunting, snuffling sound answering his own voice!

His breathing coming in terrified gasps, he

realized the saurians were still there. Their heavy footsteps told him they were on the other side of the wreckage.

He cursed himself for an idiot, still coherent enough to realize he should have kept his mouth shut. Perhaps, if they hadn't seen or heard him, they might have left.

The *Tyrannosaurus* was swifter than the others, appearing from around one corner of the wreckage, its sulfur-yellow eyes rotating in hooded sockets to fix immediately upon its prey. There was, David thought, almost a smile on those huge, sickening lips.

He raised the rifle, pain of movement making him groan, and aimed at the *Tyrannosaurus's* left eye, forcing himself to concentrate on that eye and nothing else, only that eye. . . .

It happened quickly, just as he'd been about to fire. He could feel something sucking at his mind, pulling, drawing from him that part of his being that made him human. He tried to pull the trigger but could not, could only stare into that sulfur-yellow eye. Ever so slowly, his fingers relaxed their grip on the rifle, relaxed their tremendous hold on something they had managed to retain through the length of a body-crushing fall.

The *Tyrannosaurus* moved closer, and its hot, fetid breath burning David Grimsby's nostrils with its closeness, it thrust its mighty head into the wreckage.

The saurians grunted at one another, then slowly moved away from the twisted wreckage and the mangled corpse.

CHAPTER 18

"David! He's dead!" Dian Grimsby cried. Her face was contorted, her eyes wide and glazed with shock. She stood staring at the empty screen, repeating, "He's dead" over and over in a flat monotone that was all the more dreadful for its lack of emphasis.

Bishop took her by the arms. "Hold on!" he ordered, shaking her. "Cool it! Calm down!"

She looked at him. Her eyes were empty; she spoke thickly, with one word slurring into the next. She told what she had seen, how the six saurians attacked and wrecked the train in which her husband had journeyed into the darkness of Dino-World. She went through everything with the dry, dispassionate tone she would use in delivering a scientific paper at a meeting, and except for the curious slurring of her words, she sounded perfectly controlled. She finished the account, and a moment later, shivered and was hysterical. Bishop shook her, got no response, and finally slapped her cleanly across the face with his open palm. The screams stopped abruptly, and Dian began to cry, harsh, rocking sobs. Leea, ever the empathetic spirit, put her arms around the sobbing woman, and the sobs slackened.

"Take her to the house," Bishop said. "She'll be all right in a while. I. . . ."

"Yes?" Leea asked when it became apparent Bishop would speak no more.

"I'll stay here," Bishop told her, "to replay the tape and see exactly what happened." It was possible that David was still alive, that the saurian had not managed to kill him. Dian had seen only the massive jaws *reaching* for David, had not seen them close. He reached for the playback switch.

Fifteen minutes later, he turned off the monitor, still not sure whether David Grimsby was dead or alive. At the crucial moment, the monitor had ceased taping. The angle of the recording devices had left many doubts, for it *appeared* the saurian might be unable to reach David. If that was true, the man might still be alive.

He punched the security alarm to alert the guards in the watch towers around the park and waited until the duty officer appeared in the doorway, quickly, efficiently.

"Sir?"

"David Grimsby," Bishop started, "went out in a train, and the lizards attacked him and wrecked the train. His wife thinks he's dead."

"Is he?"

"I don't know. The monitor recording stopped while he was still alive."

"Should I organize a search party?"

"No. Keep the perimeter guarded. Call the military and the police. Get reinforcements with heavy weapons.

"Very well, sir."

"Call my house and tell Leea that I'm going to investigate. It's possible that Dr. Grimsby is still alive."

"Do you want a couple of guards?"

"No. This is a one-man job. More would be in the way. I'll go because I know these beasts better than any man here. You get this place buttoned up so tight that a fly can't get out."

"Yes, sir," the duty officer said.

Bishop opened the arms rack and took out a rifle. It was a feeble weapon but he felt more secure with it in his hands.

The train, stripped to the lead car, moved into the boarding area and stopped. Bishop took a step toward it and then paused, for out of the ramp that led to the ground below came Leea. Her eyes were wide and frightened.

"No! No, Gene. Don't go! The reeka will kill you!"

"David is my friend."

"David is *dead*. There is emptiness where he used to be," Leea said. "It's no use."

"I must," Bishop said. "It's the only way." He rested his hand on her waist and pulled her toward him. She was shivering uncontrollably. "Look, honey. Don't worry about me. I'm a good shot, and unlike David, I'll be looking for trouble."

Lights flashed on around the periphery of the park. Bishop nodded. Security was going on full alert.

"I'll be back in a few minutes. If David is still alive it may take longer. But don't worry. The dinosaur that kills me hasn't been hatched yet."

"David is dead," she answered. "You need not go. It is no use."

"You don't know he's dead," Bishop said.

"I know! But if you must go, then I'll go with you."

Bishop shook his head.

Her face was as expressionless as red stone. "I *will* go with you," she intoned.

And strangely enough, it was Gene Bishop who backed down. Leea was as stubborn as anyone else, but this was different, something much more important than mere pigheadedness. Bishop knew that she would follow him on foot if he refused to let her accompany him. So it made little sense to refuse her.

"Very well," he told her simply, "come along."

A SHORT time later they were speeding above the terrain of Dino-World, and as Bishop watched the ground below, he couldn't help but feel something had been missing from his life since he'd agreed to the job here. Was this what he really wanted for himself? He didn't know.

He became aware of Leea's hand grasping his own tightly, and he returned the squeeze, never once taking his eyes off the ground. He wished, absently, that she knew how to use a blaster, but the red-skinned girl had shunned the energy weapons with the same distaste she'd displayed toward the dinosaurs.

They saw the twisted wreckage then, and the car they rode in stopped near it. In the darkness they could see little, but the sounds and Leea's sudden shiver of fear told Bishop saurians were nearby. Now that he'd become aware of the presence of at least one of them, he could detect a faint, musky odor.

"Reeka!" Leea whispered fearfully. "Think happy thoughts," she instructed Bishop. "Of love, or beauty, or a good show."

Bishop did not need to know why she had told him to think of love at a time when the exact opposite flooded through his mind. Somehow he understood that such thoughts confused the reeka, made them pass by prey they would ordinarily have slaughtered.

How do I love thee? Let me count the ways.
I love thee to the depth and breadth and height
My soul can reach, when feeling out of sight
For the ends of Being and ideal Grace
I love thee to the level of every day's
Most quiet need, by sun and candlelight
I love thee freely, as men strive for Right
I love thee purely, as they turn from praise
I love thee with the passion put to use
In my old griefs and with my childhood's faith
I love thee with a love I seemed to lose
With my lost saints—I love thee with the breath,
Smiles, tears, of all my life—and, if God choose,
I shall but love thee better after death.

He heard her sob beside him and reached out to touch her tear-wet cheek.

"How do I love thee, Gene," she whispered. "Let me count the ways."

They sat in voiceless communion, while beneath them the sounds of however many dinosaurs were present slowly died as the creatures moved away. For long moments after the last crackle of underbrush had died away, Bishop and Leea sat in the car.

Finally, Bishop stood and surveyed the terrain. There were no other saurians in the vicinity—at least, none that he could see or detect with the rifle's infrared scope. Far in the distance, however, they could hear the giant horrors bellowing, grunting.

"Reeka," Leea whispered as she stared across the moonlit space.

"Let's go," Bishop said. He opened the side door of the cab and jiggled the controls until the support tower was beside the door. He swung one foot onto the steel rings and climbed down the ferroconcrete shaft to the ground. Leea followed, demonstrating a speed and agility that probably had saved her from saurians many times on her own planet. They walked cautiously to the wreckage ahead and looked for David Grimsby. When Bishop saw the first car he wished he had not come. David was mangled almost beyond recognition. Only his head was undamaged, and his face bore such an expression of mindless peace that Bishop wanted to vomit.

"Let's go back," he said. "He's dead. We can do nothing here."

"I understand," Leea whispered. "I knew he had died. The reeka took his soul before they killed him. He felt no pain. His face is that of one whose soul has fled."

There was no reason to remain. All that was left to do was report to the park bureau. Possibly that would result in Dino-World being closed while its murderous inhabitants were examined. That it would remain closed forever was doubtful. It was too profitable and too popular. Perhaps if a substantial number of visitors were eaten, the bureau might change its mind. He shrugged. Where politicians were concerned, he'd lost his childish innocence. It was going to take real shock action to jar the bureau into action.

Leea suddenly grasped his arm. "Reeka!" she hissed, pointing toward a frighteningly familiar shape.

It was a carnosaur, a big one and as it crashed toward them through the shadows and into the moonlight, Bishop recognized it. It was *Oedipus rex*; the creature who invaded his dreams and turned them into nightmares; the beast that was so ugly of temper that it even rejected its own kind.

Bishop lifted the rifle and stepped in front of Leea. He knew their only chance at survival was a well-aimed blast that would reach the animal's brain. But now, there was now only one blaster against a beast even more gigantic than those that had absorbed the fire of four weapons as big as the one he carried.

The gigantic form came to a sudden stop. The toothy head swiveled to point at Bishop's and Leea's hiding place. Down came the wide head, its teeth bluish white in the moonbeams. The flat space between the wide-set yellow eyes came into the gun sight. Bishop's finger touched the firing stud.

The man's brain screamed "fire!" but his finger did not move—*those eyes*! A power emanated from them that paralyzed his muscles and drew his mind from his body! He battled against the weird force, trying desperately to use his weapon, but he could not move.

Staring into those eyes, he felt a part of him being sucked away. And then, he realized he was no longer a man, was no longer confined by the limits of his body. He was something beyond human, without form or matter. He was an essence!

He could no longer feel Leea behind him, nor could he feel the weight of the blaster in his hands. The essence that made him a cogent creature floated in a hazy, shapeless void. When he glanced downward to look at his body, he could see only the fading image of it lying corpselike upon the earth, with the sobbing figure of Leea bent over it.

Then there was blackness. Where was he? Was this the nonbeing philosophers had theorized over and debated in past ages? He wondered if he were alive or dead, sane or not, on a journey to heaven or hell.

Slowly, agonizingly slowly, his vision came back to him, colorless and distorted. His head, or what he thought of as his head, was unfamiliar and difficult to move. Below, far below, he could see Leea and his human body. He knew then that hands and feet moved according to his will; monstrous appendages covered with gray scales shone metallically in the moonlight. The claws were his. Taking a single step forward, he saw the birdlike left foot of a dinosaur thud into the dirt, and he felt the impact slowly and imperfectly.

As waves of horror swept over his mind and threatened to drive him mad, he knew he was now locked inside the skull of the saurian.

Gene Bishop was *Oedipus rex*!

CHAPTER 19

Bishop somehow sensed that the body he inhabited held another besides himself, a being that transcended the limits of space and time. He stared through the yellow eyes of the saurian onto an alien landscape and his mind received a liturgy. . . .

I scan the splendid horror of this world—not the one on which I stand or the one that I have left but the world that existed . when we first came—a world where hordes of saurians of myriad shapes and sizes move across its surface; only the cunning remain alive. Hungry predators battle each other beneath the twin suns to satisfy their territorial imperative, and to compete for the savory flesh of their prey.

This is a world where only those capable of survival can survive—a world of hunting, of blood-splashed conflict where flesh-eater bites the throat of flesh-eater for possession of a carcass . . . where plant-eaters without protective armament must learn to run to avoid their perpetually hungry stalkers.

This is a world of ancient heedless cruelty—a violent world, where life and death are but a jaw's width apart, a world of jaws and hungry bellies that clamor to be filled, a world that continually resounds with the squeaks and bellows of the dying.

Time moves. Behold the night. . . .

Uncountable saurian heads gaze toward the starry sky, and the streaks brighten the heavens; I am a part of those brilliant swaths. I have no flesh. I live, I think, I dwell within burning crystals thrown into space when my home world shudders, explodes and dies. There is nothing my race can do to prevent the catastrophe, for we are vortices of energy and thought, capable of little save cognizance and crystallization.

Many of us do not survive the burning atmosphere through which we plunge. Those of us who are not destroyed—a pitiful few—break from our crystalline prisons. We stream freely through the warm winds of this, our new home, seeking an alternate existence to the one that doomed us on our native world.

Solidity, we learn, is necessary for survival. So we seek the primary life forms of this life-filled world—creatures of impressive size and strength that multiply with startling rapidity. These animals we seek and their small brains are suited to our needs. Within their titanic bodies are the tactile and locomotive powers we require. And those of us who survive our world's doom commandeer the animals. We become one with them, a symbiosis wherein they provide the body while we supply the ability to think and plan and dominate the minds of lesser creatures.

Yet once we merge we are trapped, unable to free ourselves from these living prisons. Truly, since there are no other creatures upon this world to oppose us, we do well with our entrapment. Every creature that hatches from our muddy eggs propagates another of our kind—to motivate the body, to communicate with others of our kind, to *pass along the memories of our past without the slightest loss.*

As on our long-dead planet, we bear no hatred toward each other, for our minds are attuned and we share our intellects. We have no need to inflict harm upon each other. But now, in our assumed forms, there is conflict. The flesh-eaters among us wish to eat those who are not flesh-eaters and destroy that feeling of fraternity that exists among us. Although we are now predator and prey we train our new bodies to not molest others of our kind, nor seek to slay as had been done prior to our arrival.

Therefore, we who eat flesh hunger.

Unable to prey upon our kind, we seek the smaller life forms to satisfy our bodies' needs. When the warm-blooded creatures dawn upon this world, we devour them, entrancing them first with the strength of our minds so that little violence is required to acquire food. And during the millenium upon millenium that follow, we prosper.

Time blurs forward, and our days are at peace with our time. Creatures with intelligence are born. Though they think and plan and communicate audibly with each other, their minds are weak and receptive to our control. We prey upon these more ferociously than on the other mammals, for long ago we envisioned the evolutionary ladder of this world and know that beings with brains will someday dominate all others.

The world is altering. The days get colder. New vegetation replaces that upon which the herbi-

vores among us feed. Our refusal to attack and devour others of our kind contributes to the food shortage. Perhaps we may someday discover new food sources, but there are problems.

The human beings grow more clever with each passing year. Though we regulate their actions if we confront them, the creatures learn to evade us . . . to move from tree to tree, from cave to cave. Their smaller, swifter bodies often flee before we can entrance them with our gaze. And these creatures devise weapons, so now we must compete with them in preying upon the smaller life forms.

We are doomed to extinction. But the most deadly contributor to our doom is ourselves; for when we originally traversed space in crystal form we brought with us a virus, harmless to what we were, but deadly to what we are. It kills us in increasing numbers and relatively few of our kind survive to maturity.

Our hunger grows.

Our numbers shrink.

In time we shall become extinct unless an alternative is provided.

The alternative comes from the stars. A craft bearing beings similar to the mammal bipeds we hunt descends with a promise of new life. We read the motivations of the craft's occupants. We know they intend to transport our eggs to their world . . . we know that the virus that exists in the atmosphere of this world is unknown on theirs. We know that nothing must deter them from taking us to this new life.

We are born anew on this, our third world-

home, fully aware of that which has preceded us. We are free of the fatal virus. We shall strive to preserve our species. We shall endure!

But do we have the right to destroy another intelligent race? I alone now realize the immorality of preserving our species at the expense of another. But I cannot halt—

And then Bishop was extruded; he floated, descended and once more inhabited his body. The cold ground pressed against his back and Leea was tugging at him, attempting to pull him away from the giant carnosaur.

Head aching, Bishop raised his eyes toward the towering predator. Yet as his vision focused upon the mass of muscles, talons and teeth, he perceived the probable reason for his hasty ejection.

"Reeka!" exclaimed Leea.

They were slowly advancing, a slightly smaller carnosaur accompanied by a *Trachodon* and an *Ankylosaurus*. The armored dinosaur was turning toward the two humans. It brought its tail about with startling speed.

He could imagine Leea behind him, immobilized by the saurians' power and standing transfixed as she had on that alien riverbank. But to Bishop's astonishment, she continued to drag him out of range of that monstrous tail so that it slammed harmlessly against the ground rather than smashing apart his head. None of the creatures had yet focused upon the woman. All except the *Ankylosaurus* were fascinated by the bellowing *Tyrannosaurus* who stood between them and the humans.

Again the heavy tail swung. Again it missed. This action seemed a bluff, an attempt to try to intimidate their unexpected guardian.

Oedipus rex continued standing his ground, challenging them—his body and tail were parallel to the ground, his forelimbs clawed the air. The other dinosaurs rumbled, trying to find an opening, yet not possessing the courage to fight even if an opening were presented. They watched the king's strange behavior, their yellow eyes glowing in the darkness. Then tired of the confrontation they turned away, and lumbered back from where they had come.

The two humans vanished into the shadowy depths of the woods and ran toward the caves in the cliffside. Reaching one cave, they stood in its mouth, their lungs heaving from exertion. In the distance they heard continued bellowing. And then, before them, the remaining dinosaur, the carnosaur, appeared striding back and forth before the caves, its mouth dripping saliva—as though it could already enjoy the taste of human flesh.

CHAPTER 20

Bishop watched the brute as it paced back and forth. "It seems we're back on Erigon," he murmured.

"It knows we are here somewhere," Leea said. "Soon it will search for us. If it finds us, it will draw us as that reeka drew you." She shook her head. "I do not know why we were not eaten. Your soul was gone, and I could not leave you."

"That one is our friend," Bishop said.

She shook her head. "Reeka are friends of no one except each other. On Erigon that one would have sucked us into his jaws. This one outside would eat us if he knew where we were. Let us go to the back of this cave and generate defense so it cannot sense us. They do not know love and thoughts of it make them feel empty and uneasy."

"Under the circumstances, thoughts of love are farthest from my mind," Bishop murmured.

"You must think them. Our lives depend on it." Her eyes were wide, the pupils inky pools.

"Do you love me?" she asked.

"As I love—no more than I love—life."

"Then show it. Hold me, my darling. Make my thoughts warm with the love of you. Otherwise we will die." She laid her hand upon his arm and led him back into the depths of the cave. They huddled there with their arms about each other, drawing warmth and comfort from each other's nearness.

Bishop felt by turns tender, protective and possessive. All the strange magic Leea could generate in him was aroused as he held her close, kissed her and felt her respond.

"Oh Gene," she sighed. Her voice was ghost faint in the darkness. She touched him tenderly. Her mind was filled with love and she was secure in the circle of his arms.

They didn't speak. They laid there breast to breast, drawing comfort from each other, lost in the wonder of sensations that were only peripherally sexual.

And outside, the carnosaur turned away from the mouth of a vacant cave that held nothing except the scent of mammals that had passed through it. There was nothing alive in there. To the beast and the thing that rode within it, the cave was empty.

Bishop lay quietly. He wasn't conscious that the saurian had gone. His mind was filled with Leea. She was more than any man deserved. He touched her softly and her hand crept into his. Then, suddenly, she stirred.

"The reeka is gone, Gene," she stated. "We should go too."

She was right but he had no desire to move.

"We should go back," Leea said.

He sighed. He knew what would happen when he returned. In his mind's eye, he could see the stack of forms, papers and reports he would have to fill out. Bureaus are never satisfied with telephone or video calls.

A vagrant thought stirred his mind. Perhaps the park bureau would be more responsive if he could tell them what the saurians were doing. The thought excited him.

If Grimsby had died because of the saurian's desire for secrecy, it must be important. He was rationalizing and he knew it, but he didn't wish to go back to the questions and paperwork.

He told Leea what he wanted to do.

She objected.

He told her to go back, that he would go alone.

She said no.

And so they both went into Desolation World. It was a triumph of stupidity over common sense, but of such things are heroes—and corpses—made. They were unarmed; their only light was the moon. But they moved north into the wilderness, and from somewhere ahead came the grumbling noises of the giant saurians.

The land had an appropriate name, Leea thought. Vegetation was virtually nonexistent, and the terrain was rough and broken and filled with rocky masses and shadows. It was a wilderness in the harshest and most elemental sense. And as they moved into the area, the saurian noises grew in volume.

Leea wished she had the unquenchable optimism of her mate. Already he had forgotten that he should have been eaten. He was sublimely confident that in this terrain they could outrun any saurian. In her book success was a poor assumption. She knew reeka and their devilishness. But for the moment Bishop was beyond reason. He was in the grip of an excitement for which he had no name. She could feel it, but she didn't understand it. But then—neither did Bishop.

Finally, they reached the summit of the last

ridge that separated them from the dinosaurs. As they peered down into the valley, the plan became disquietingly obvious. Now he knew what the dinosaurs did each night when they went beyond the range of the video cameras.

All of them were there, scaly hides highlighted by the pallid moon glow. No, Bishop corrected himself, they weren't *all* there. One was missing. He counted twenty-nine of the brutes, all grunting and bellowing in cacophonous concert. Nowhere did he perceive the huge carnosaur that had pulled him into its parasitic mind.

Fourteen of the dinosaurs were performing egg dances. Beneath them, almost green in the moonlight, lay a field of eggs—hundreds, perhaps thousands of ovoid shapes, spread across the earth like some lumpy carpet. All the eggs required was time and heat. Before long they would hatch, while the saurians would continue to mate and deposit more eggs on their adopted soil. And the little ones were small enough to slip through the security barriers!

"Never have I seen so many reeka," said Leea, just loud enough to be heard above the noises coming from below. "On my world, the reeka lay many eggs, but not so many as these!"

"It doesn't take a paleontologist to see what's going on here," Bishop said grimly as he watched the dinosaurs. "I'll bet the plan is to put us up to our ears in alligators!" These monstrosities could create panic and death among humanity before they were exterminated.

There was perplexity in Leea's eyes, for empathy was no substitute for words and she could not communicate telepathically as did the saurians. She could only receive vague images.

"They were dying on Erigon," she said. "There was a sickness that killed their young."

Bishop nodded. "I know," he said. "The reeka told me."

"But on my world the reeka rule. Why should they want to be taken here where they are few and weak."

"They don't think they'll be few and weak. And they don't know how many of us there are. On Earth, they reason that they might have a better chance to survive. Our air is free of the virus that is killing them on Erigon."

Leea moved forward, closer to the edge to get a better view of the eggs. "Why do they lay so many eggs?"

Bishop now saw that some of the eggs had already hatched. Infant saurians were crawling about the remnants of their eggshells. "Leea, don't you see? They come here at night to secretly lay as many eggs as possible, to hatch out hordes of young that can pass through our electronic fences while they are small and escape into the forests. Then, when their offspring are numerous and strong enough, they'll begin to spread across the Earth. They won't succeed, of course, but they'll try to take over and many people will be killed before the last of them are destroyed."

"Can they . . . can they do this thing?" asked Leea with fear in her large eyes.

"I doubt it," Bishop said. "They could not have learned of human history and our knowledge of weaponry. No dinosaur is a match for an anti-tank missile or a well-aimed bomb. But they must try; it's their only chance for survival."

"It is good to kill them now," Leea said.

Bishop's thoughts were abruptly terminated by the flash of a blast rifle that traced white destruction through the darkness, incinerating a cluster of eggs. An armored female in the laying dance lifted her tiny head and shrieked. Instantly the other monsters were alert. Bishop realized with amazement that the gunner was Dian Grimsby. She was standing to his left and below the ridge, the rifle awkwardly clutched in her hands. Her face was a pale blob in the moonlight. Her eyes were wide, her mouth contorted in a grimace of hate. She fired again and incinerated a few more eggs. It was a futile gesture, Bishop thought. One gun couldn't make a dent in this depository. He stood up, waved and yelled.

Dian turned. She saw them and waved.

"Get out of there!" Bishop yelled.

"No! I owe them this." She leveled the blaster and fired again. The rational scientist had become the emotional avenger.

Bishop sighed. There was nothing he could do. Her position was untenable. If she moved now she could get away before the saurians could reach her. If she waited much longer, they would get her.

"Filthy beasts!" Dian screamed and loosed a fourth blast. This one caught the eye of the Stegosaur whose eggs she destroyed. The beast screamed its pain into the night and fell upon its eggs. The heavy spiked tail beat up and down, crushing dozens of the leathery receptacles.

The activity ceased. A beast roared. Another grunted, and in a body they turned on Dian.

"Run!" Bishop bellowed.

But Dian did not hear or heed. She continued to fire, destroying eggs as the saurians advanced. She wasted no shots on the adults. The blast that killed the stegosaur was sheer luck and she knew it. She simply wanted to kill saurians. Their size was not important.

"She will die," said Leea. "The reeka will get her." It was a statement of obvious fact. "I shall weep for her spirit."

The monsters were nearly upon Dian as she stood her ground and kept firing into the eggs and hatching young. There was something incredibly brave and futile about it, and Bishop could feel the breath catch in his throat as he watched. In a tiny way she was humanity, thumbing its nose at destruction for one last shot at the enemy. At the end, her courage faltered as the moon shadows of the saurians fell upon her. She turned to run and stumbled on the rocky slope.

Bishop cursed. He could not stand by idly and watch another death . . . he had to do *something*! It was insane, stupid, foolhardy and in the best human tradition.

But fast as Bishop was, he was not nearly fast enough. A huge saurian head bit through Dian's body. Dark smears appeared as Dian screamed.

He stopped, sick with hatred and frustration. This death was worse than either of the others.

A crimson shape ran past him. With a bravery Bishop had never imagined, Leea scooped up the blast rifle and scrambled out of the path of the saurian. "Here!" she called as she ran to him. "Kill the reeka!"

Bishop grabbed the weapon from her hands. The saurian was already upon them. The others followed like a grim procession of primordial executioners. Without thought, Bishop blasted at the head of the leader, an act that didn't slow the brute a bit as energy tore at the thick skin and bone and missed the brain.

"Come on!" Bishop shouted, grasped Leea's wrist and pulled her away. "We can run faster. We'll get away."

They turned up the slope and scrambled toward the top—and then they froze. Their escape was blocked by yet another saurian—a carnosaur that stood tall and majestic, silhouetted against the moon. The animal's bulk was a gigantic black pillar against the sky, and suddenly Bishop recognized it. It was the wayward one.

The great mouth opened as Bishop pulled Leea up the slope. A roar, higher pitched and more urgent, came from the distended jaws. The massive walking legs of *Oedipus rex* began to move; the tail lashed from side to side. Muscles bulged beneath scaly hide as this most awesome of all terrestrial flesh-eaters thundered down the slope toward the twenty-eight surviving dinosaurs. The horde was shocked at their kin's aggression, and for a moment they froze with indecision. It was enough. Bishop pulled Leea up the slope and over the rim as the rebel *Tyrannosaurus* stalked into the saurians below.

They didn't hesitate. The attack was met by

furious fangs and ripping horns. As Bishop and Leea reached the top of the ridge, they witnessed the *Tyrannosaurus* biting into the leading adversary with his powerful jaws, shearing the throat. A second clamp of those dreadful jaws severed the head. The decapitated body fell, its taloned feet flailing helplessly in the air.

The victorious saurian screamed defiance and moved onward toward the armored might of a *Triceratops*. The massive theropod managed to avoid the horns and rip his adversary's belly and guts with his fangs. The others swarmed upon him, biting, striking and battering, and Oedipus was knocked from his feet and buried under tons of angry flesh.

Bishop and Leea were forgotten; they dashed for the monorail. They did not pause until they were aboard the train and it was running, full speed in reverse, back to the park entrance.

The noises of saurian madness still resounded faintly as they reached the tower. Leea and Gene looked upon each other and sighed.

"What do we do now?" Leea asked.

"Call the board. Call the military," Bishop said.

There would be little trouble in getting the park bureau to take the necessary action. The evidence was clear enough. Two dead humans, a valley filled with eggs and the neurosynthesizer record of what had happened to him in his encounter with the carnosaur would be more than enough.

Extending his hand to Leea, Bishop helped her

to her feet. Slowly, they walked down the passageway to their home. And on the way, Leea touched him and smiled.

How long had it been since he had seen her smile? It was still the same night that David had gone out to die, but it seemed as though a year had passed.

Einstein was right, he thought inconsequentially. Everything was relative. Kiss a girl and an hour seems like a minute; sit on a hot stove and a minute seems like a year. He sighed. He was tired of sitting on hot stoves. There should be faster ways of passing time.

CHAPTER 21

It took nearly two weeks before the scene was set and the materials assembled. Boards and commissions met and decided that for Earth's safety, the reeka must be destroyed. Since it was impossible to destroy the reeka without killing their hosts, the dinosaurs, too, must perish.

Meanwhile, the electronic fences were strengthened, and police contingents armed with blasters and riot gas patrolled the walls that kept the saurians confined. The reeka knew that something had gone wrong. Hundreds of new-hatched saurians tried to slip through the fences and past the guards, but were caught and killed.

And finally the formalities were ended and the extermination begun. The slaughter commenced at precisely 08:00 local time and by 12:00 it was over. Bishop watched it with mixed emotions. It was satisfying, and it was sickening, and he didn't know which feeling was dominant. Leea was at his side, delighting in the destruction of her enemies.

Throughout Earth, video screens were alive with death as Dino-World was destroyed with twenty-first century military technology. It was the greatest show since the final battles of World War III when the Peace of Exhaustion had ended the conflict, and the media made the most of it.

The overkill was deliberately designed to be a grim reminder of the horrors of war, but oddly, it failed in its purpose. For humanity did not relate to the dragons and viewed their death with interested indifference, especially since they knew

what the saurians harbored. It made Bishop won
der why so many had come to see the park in the
first place.

And this hellish holocaust, Bishop though
wryly, was the sort of thing men were embroiled
in less than two centuries ago. For the weapon
were museum pieces, carefully preserved exhibit
taken from the military memorials. The whol
carefully staged show was designed to show th
horror and the waste of war to generations tha
had never seen battle; for since the general peac
of 2010 was proclaimed to a war-sick world
men had fought no more.

Leea was horrified at the violence and happ
with the results. The reeka were gone. She coul
not sense a single sign of their presence. For th
first time in her life, that part of her mind wa
empty.

"No more reeka," she said. "My soul is clea
of them. But how dreadfully you Earthme
fight!"

"We're a hard race," Bishop agreed, "and w
still love violence. We conquered this world th
hard way and racial memories die hard." H
sighed. "I wonder if this show was an objec
lesson or a spectacle. Anyway, I hope my bosse
will learn a lesson from this and will think twic
before they bring any more exotic life to Eart
without investigating it thoroughly."

He was interrupted by the buzzing of his phon
alarm. He picked up a nearby phone. "Bisho
here," and then paused. "No, sir, she detects noth
ing. I believe they're all dead." Then there wa
another long pause until Bishop clipped, "No, si

Definitely not. I don't give a damn if your whole committee thinks it's safe. I wouldn't touch it with tongs!" He hung up and turned to Leea.

"I think we'll be looking for a new job," he said. "As far as wildlife parks are concerned, we've had it. That was the park bureau, and they want us to go back to Erigon to get more dinosaur eggs."

"More reeka? Why?" Leea's voice was puzzled.

"Someone in the Bureau of Research and Development thinks the reeka can be destroyed with ultrasound without damaging the saurian genes. They want to try stocking the park again if it works."

"Fools," Leea said.

"They want you to monitor the eggs for reeka."

"Smart," Leea said. That would work. I know reeka."

Bishop eyed her curiously.

"Do they offer us something for what we do for them?" she asked innocently.

"Oh, sure. The fellow said something about an independent command of a survey ship and talked about sending a punitive force to sanitize Erigon and kill off all the reeka-infested lizards, once we've gotten enough clean eggs to stock a new park."

"And you said no to that?"

Bishop nodded. "You've suffered enough. I'm not about to put you through any more. And besides, that world has killed three of my friends. How many more must I lead to their deaths?"

"That world, or the reeka in it," Leea said

quietly, "has killed many more than three of my folk. My two sisters, my baby brother, my father, my father's brother, my mate before you—all have fallen to the reeka. Probably by now my mother is dead. We do not live long on Erigon. If it were not for you I would be eaten. Your people can kill reeka. I have seen it. You can make my home safe for my folk."

"Oh, we can kill them all right. We're very efficient at killing things that are in our way. We can even kill intelligent life. We nearly exterminated dolphins on this world and they're more intelligent than we are."

"Are they reeka?"

"No, they're friendly. They like us."

"I think you are wrong not to take the park bureau offer," Leea said. "We could free my people and keep yours amused. A saurian without reeka would not be dangerous. Can you think of anything better to do?"

Bishop didn't answer. He eyed her curiously. What had happened to the clinging vine, the timid runner who fled from the very mention of reeka? Was this the same woman he had wedded and bedded? As he looked at her he saw the difference. She was somehow straighter, taller, more alive. She had been fascinating before, but she was thrilling now! With such a woman he could run the star trails forever! The bureau did offer him independent command of the expedition and held out the prospect of a survey ship if he were successful. And he wanted to get back into space. That was his proper place.

"Would you really want to go back to Erigon?" he asked.

She nodded. She could feel his love and concern, and she was content. He was her man, her mate, and he was asking her for a decision. She smiled faintly. At last he had come to sharing. It was good that she was persistent.

Now they could do much together. For she had felt his boredom and the surge of joy that filled him when they had gone into Dino-World together. They had been two against a world when they went into the desolation to discover what the reeka planned.

He would never be happy in a safe and secure job. Nor would she. This Earth was beautiful, but it was boring. There was nothing real to do. In a way it was better to fight the reeka. There was danger there, but with Earth weapons she would not be afraid; fear, she thought, was part of the saurian dominance.

She wondered what had happened to her fear. It had gone somewhere during that agonizing moment when she decided to go with her man into the terrors of Dino-World. And the fear had vanished completely when the reeka took him into it. She could face the saurians now. She could bring Earth weapons to Erigon and teach her people how to use them. And once the Earthmen had begun the program to free Erigon of reeka, her folk could do the rest.

In the last analysis, it was *her* folk who must kill them. For they must overcome their fears and kill their dragons, or else they were not fit to be free. Her folk had run too long. It was time to fight.

Her eyes glowed and her heart beat faster as she envisioned the folk of Erigon, armed with Earth weapons, joined together in bands no reeka could control, working as a team to rid their world of the intruders, the killers who had decimated their numbers over the years.

She looked at Bishop, a glint of speculation in her eyes. She wondered if he would tire of her, if he would drop her as he must have dropped other women in the past. And then she smiled. No, she knew him. And she had confidence that the two of them would grow old together.

She paused. Strange, she told herself. I have never thought of age before now. None of my folk are wrinkled and feeble. The reeka ate them long before advanced age could set in.

But she had seen old people here on Earth. They seemed happy. The mistakes of earlier ages were abolished. People could become old with dignity and purpose. It must be a wonderful thing to be old and wise with years.

She held Bishop's arm tightly. In the time ahead, they would have many adventures—on Erigon and other worlds. They would go into strange jungles together. They would cross heat-baked plains. They would submerge beneath emerald waters. And at the end of all this, after the years of strength and stamina had passed, they would sit quietly back, content with their memories and their grandchildren.

EPILOGUE

The twin suns of Erigon had risen and were full in the sky when a thunderclap of sound split the silence of the marsh. A long-necked, blue-skinned marsh dweller lifted its eyes from the coolness of the swamp, scanning the sky for the cause of the sound.

Something passed over him, shining brighter than the two suns, reflecting light from its metal sides, hurtling through the atmosphere to a place some distance from the marsh dweller's location.

The marsh dweller knew fear, then hot, scalding terror, for it had sensed something within the metallic confines of the starship, could feel the determination and resolve of those on board.

The panic rose, and the marsh dweller began to move as quickly as it could through the mud and reeds, searching for others of its kind, already broadcasting to them the tremendous danger that had come.

Extermination!

And the part of the marsh dweller that was not animal knew its warnings were in vain. The others of its kind would hear and attempt to defend themselves, but there was little hope for them.

The panic built still more, and the marsh dweller charged through the swamp, terrified, knowing there would be a battle, and knowing which side would be victorious.

High in a tree, a man who had been running for more than seven days saw the starship. He wondered what it was, for he had never seen such a thing before, but he had little time to ponder the matter; the reeka were close behind him. Before he could consider mysterious objects in the sky, he must save his life.

Why, the terrified man wondered, could he not have plucked the silver thing from the sky and hurled it against the reeka?